Slow Hope

Slow Hope

Anita Swanson

www.ivyhousebooks.com

PUBLISHED BY IVY HOUSE PUBLISHING GROUP
5122 Bur Oak Circle, Raleigh, NC 27612
United States of America
919-782-0281
www.ivyhousebooks.com

ISBN: 1-57197-435-0
Library of Congress Control Number: 2004109106

Printed in the United States of America

To Kim, Tina and 'G', who fill my heart with endless joy, pride and love.

Table of Contents

Prologue

She knew it was over as soon as her second child was born. However, by that time she was barely able to complete a thought, let alone organize a plan for getting out of her marriage. So she just let herself drift, until finally nothing seemed to matter very much at all.

She still went to church, of course. Sundays she sang at the Baptist church where her husband served as Minister of Music and Thursdays, even though her husband told her he didn't approve, she attended a Presbyterian Bible Study for women.

And she still prayed. She prayed for guidance and understanding. She prayed for wisdom and forgiveness. She prayed for help and endurance. But mostly she simply prayed for deliverance. She wanted out. Out of the bonds of her fundamental marriage. Out of her feelings of oppression. And out of the black hole that now surrounded her with every breath she took.

But praying didn't help. Eventually, she became convinced that God didn't care about her. Not really.

Despair turned from an occasional visitor into a constant companion. On her dark days she thought she could be losing her mind.

On her bright days, and there were some, she wondered if somewhere there might be a lost and found department for her sanity.

Only once in all of her despair did she call her mother.

"Mother, I need to tell you something."

"You're not calling me with bad news, are you, Anne?"

Her shoulders sagged. "I just wanted you to know that things aren't going very well."

Her mother said nothing.

"Please, Mother. It's been really hard for me lately."

"Life is hard. Life is always hard. But we all just make the best of it, now don't we? I don't want to hear any more. You've told me enough. You've made your bed, now you're going to have to lie in it."

She hung up the phone. Her despair increased. Time began to drag on forever.

Friends would call and inquire, but she couldn't admit to them how desperate she was. She couldn't even admit it to herself. How was she ever going to admit it to her friends?

And then one day in the middle of the produce aisle of the grocery store, she lost track of why she was there.

It took forty-five minutes to purchase three small items and when she got home, she couldn't figure out how to get the small brown paper bag containing the bread, milk, and a box of Pampers into the house.

If someone had told her she was depressed, she would've denied it. To her it was an energy problem. She simply didn't have enough.

"I don't think things can get much worse," she said as she sat and stared out the car window, trying to understand how all of this could've happened simply because she loved music.

Chapter One

Music. It was Always About the Music

"Do you know how to sing a scale?" was all he asked. No introduction. No small talk. Not even the standard audition request of "So, tell me a little about yourself."

I nodded my head and he began playing a C major scale. "Follow along and let me hear how you sound." His fingers glided easily over the keys of the black Steinway. "Sing me an E," he called out as he quickly changed from scales into a C major chord.

My voice sounded confident but I was nervous. My gaze shifted from his fingers to the clock on the wall above his head.

He changed chords. "Can you pick out an A in this one?"

I sang an A.

Once again he changed chords. "Fine, fine. Now, listen carefully and give me a G."

I sang a G.

"Great. Well, that's it," he said as he stood up, clapped his hands together, and glanced up at the clock. "I don't need to hear any more."

"That's it?" My voice trembled. Panic had already set in. "You don't want to hear any more? I can sing a solo if you want. I've got one all ready."

He shook his head. "No. I don't need to hear it. You'll be fine."

"Does this mean I didn't make it?"

He smiled. "No. You have a nice voice. You'll be a great asset to the choir." He didn't sound rude, just matter-of-fact. "Would you send the next girl in when you leave?"

I couldn't move. Was that all there was to it?

He looked at me and smiled. "Yes?" It was more of a statement than a question. "That's it. You did great."

I tried to smile but already my lip was quivering. "Okay then." I nodded my head, turned and walked out the door.

The next girl waiting in the hallway was someone I'd met at freshman orientation. "What's he like?" she asked with nervous enthusiasm. "I heard he makes the audition really fun!"

I shrugged my shoulders, swallowed hard to keep from crying and stooped down to retrieve my books from the worn beige linoleum floor. "I don't think he liked me very much," I said. "All he asked me do was sing a scale and pick some notes out of a chord."

"Do you think you made it in?"

"Yeah, he said I did. You'd better go in. He's waiting for you and I think he's in a hurry. I'll see you back at the dorm."

My audition was over and I'd been accepted into the student nurses' choir. I should have been ecstatic. But I wasn't.

I'd been counting on the choir audition to do what music had always done for my short seventeen-year-old life: save me.

Music. It was always about music.

I can't remember a time when music wasn't as important to me as breathing. I hear melodies in the rain. Symphonies sing in my head. Handel flows through my heart, Rossini and Puccini through my soul.

It began when my Sunday school teacher asked me to sing "Away in a Manger" in the church Christmas pageant. In rehearsal I did it perfectly, but on the night of the performance with my five-year-old heart bursting with excitement, I stumbled over the words in the second verse. Even so, by the time I'd finished the traditional Christmas hymn and the applause had died out, I knew I could sing. And in that flickering moment of time, my life-long love affair with music was born.

For the next six years I sang constantly. I sang in choirs at our neighborhood Lutheran church and choirs at school. I sang to myself and to anyone who'd listen. I dreamed up musicals and produced them in neighborhood basements.

But it all came to an abrupt end one day after school when my mother, weary of my never-ending musical concert, yelled up the stairs through my closed bedroom door. "Anne, will you just shut up? I'm sick of hearing you sing all the time!"

Like erupting molten lava, her words burned their way into my heart as I calmly sat on my twin bed and picked the loose threads on my blue cotton chenille bedspread.

I kept the door closed. I didn't want to hear my mother's voice let alone look at her.

I cleared my throat and fought back the tears. I was determined she was never going to see me cry. "Why don't you ever say anything to Sherry and Jane when they sing?" I said, convinced that my voice had not betrayed my secret pain.

"Because your sisters have lovely voices, that's why. All the ladies in my church circle even said so. Besides, your new band director called yesterday and asked if we'd let you play a school instrument. They have something called an oboe. He said it was one of the most difficult instruments to play. I told him you were pretty good in music and I'd go along with anything to get you to stop singing." And then she laughed. "So I guess it's the oboe or nothing."

I opened the door. "What's an oboe?"

"Anne, if you want to do it, tell your teacher. They're supposed to take care of everything."

I didn't care what I had to do to keep music in my life. If I had to learn how to play one of the most difficult instruments in the band, then that is what I would do. I went to the band room in my elementary school the very next day.

Fortunately for me, I fell in love with the oboe and it saved my musical life. Fascinated by its lonely, haunting sound, I practiced constantly.

Six months later when the band director asked my parents if I could study with the principal oboist from the Minneapolis Symphony, they astonished me by saying "yes."

But it wasn't only the oboe that sang its siren song to me. The day my mother returned to the hospital to resume a full-time position in nursing, I was set free.

Free to blast my forty-five records on our small green plastic phonograph in the corner of the basement, and free to belt out the latest hits by everyone from Theresa Brewer to Doris Day to Kay Star. When Elvis came onto the scene a whole new set of fantasies took over my adolescent musical life. With all the earnestness a twelve-year-old girl could muster, I practiced his hip gyrating movements and dreamed of the time when Elvis would sing his love songs just for me.

With each passing day music drew me deeper and deeper

in until it saturated my entire life. By the time I reached my senior year in high school, I had convinced myself that someday I would be a famous singer or at the very least an oboist in the Minnesota Orchestra. From that point on I decided to dedicate the rest of my life to music. I knew my parents would not be pleased, but still I thought I could garner their support. I was wrong.

"Ridiculous, Anne. This is absolutely ridiculous," was my mother's terse response. "You know perfectly well you're going to be our nurse."

I fought back. "You don't own me, you know, and it just so happens I don't want to be a nurse."

"Stop talking nonsense. Of course you want to be a nurse. I've known you were going to be the one to follow in my footsteps since the day you were born. Go ask your father if you still don't believe me. He was the first person I told."

My cherished dreams evaporated with every word she spoke, and still I fought on. "Just because you love nursing doesn't mean that I will."

"Be as nasty as you want. Your father and I are in complete agreement on this. We're not going to give you a dime for your college education unless you become a nurse. Besides, he intends to have a talk with you."

Suddenly I felt my heart play leap frog deep from within in my chest. I hated to be forewarned of an impending discussion with my father. My father never discussed anything. He talked. You listened. And it was never good.

"About what?"

"About the excellent program the army has for student nurses."

That evening I stared at my father in defeat. "You want me to join the army because they'll pay my tuition, right?"

My father said nothing. His silence told me everything I needed to know.

"Well, I'm not going to join the army. I'll get a job this summer and earn my own tuition to nursing school if that's what it takes for me to get out of this house, but there's absolutely no way you're going to make me join the army."

"Fine, then. It's settled."

And it was.

Two months later, I returned my school-owned oboe to an empty band room and headed out to the football field where, along with the other three hundred and sixty-four of my classmates, I graduated.

That fall I entered Minnesota Hospital's School of Nursing in Minneapolis.

I chose Minnesota not only because they had accepted me in spite of my unexceptional grades, but also because of an intriguing sentence in their school brochure. "Our student nurses choir," it read, "is highly respected for its level of community involvement and is directed by the internationally known choir director, Bob Mansfield."

If I have to go to nursing school, I thought, *at least I'm going to go to one that has a choir.*

But I was overwhelmed from the start. Science courses, a consistent problem for me in high school, continued to plague me and with each lecture I fell further and further behind. Too ashamed to admit to anyone I was in trouble, I told no one and before the quarter was out I was already drowning in a sea of potential academic disaster.

In desperation, I reached out to my roommate Ilene, who from that moment on became my tutor, my confidant, my lifesaver and friend. Science made sense to Ilene and with her help it soon began to make sense to me. I did not soar to the top of the class, but I did accomplish one extraordinary event: I passed. And through it all, music remained my one solitary joy and comfort.

As a child the sound of my own voice lifted in song had the power to boost my self-confidence and give me hope. It continued to do so during that long difficult freshman year.

• • •

The year I turned five and sang "Away in a Manager" in church, Bob had just turned twenty-two and was already under the mentorship of the famous choral conductor Robert Shaw.

By the time our paths crossed at the choir audition in the fall of 1961, Bob was thirty-four years old and considered by many to be the most successful choir director and entertainer the state of Minnesota had ever produced. He was, by reputation, charismatic, funny and famous.

The public adored him. He also happened to be the Minister of Music of the largest Methodist church in Minneapolis—and married.

The student nurse's choir wasn't scheduled to begin rehearsing until three weeks into the fall semester, and even though I knew I hadn't made much of an impression on Bob at my audition, I was eager for rehearsals to begin. *Somehow,* I thought as I walked into the choir room on the night of our first rehearsal, *this man will live up to his vast reputation and I can prove myself to him.*

He did. Where once he'd been distant and distracted, he now oozed with charm and told jokes. Where he'd been abrupt, he was now patient. Questions from choir members were treated with respect and humor. Difficult passages of music he made easy. The easy music he made fun.

It was a curious observation to many of the student nurses that he didn't look much like a traditional choir director. Standing six feet tall, he had thick, wavy, and unruly black hair. His dark brown eyes sparkled constantly with mischief. And he was big. During rehearsal I heard one classmate gush, "Too bad he's built just like a linebacker. He'd be so handsome if only he were thinner."

But I thought he was handsome just the way he was. "I think he looks like a giant teddy bear," I whispered to no one in particular. "A giant teddy bear come to life."

By the end of the first rehearsal, I was committed to Bob and the choir completely. Over the next few months I grew to love his constant stream of jokes and the laughter that surrounded him. I adored his energetic directing and the sound of his voice. It wasn't long before every note he sang literally wrapped itself around my heart. I wanted him to notice me. I ached to impress him. But even though I sang with great passion, arrived for rehearsals early and often found a reason to stay late, nothing seemed to work.

He was always overscheduled, and as I'd already discovered at my audition, when he was out of time he was out of charm.

There were a couple of times he took notice of me, but it was only as he was handing out music to choir. The questions he asked, "Where are you from?" or "How do you like nursing?" were nothing more than passing, courteous and social.

He certainly never gave me any indication that he was aware of me at all, which is why I was surprised and apprehensive when in March of my sophomore year, he asked me to stay after rehearsal.

"I want to ask you something," he said.

I watched as one by one the choir members said goodnight. Soon the room was empty. "You're going to ask me to leave the choir, aren't you?"

He looked confused. "Leave the choir?"

I started to stammer. "Because . . . because I missed the last two performances. Look, I had to work and I couldn't get . . ." I stopped and stared at the quizzical look on his face. "Wait a minute. I'll bet you didn't even notice I was missing. Did you?"

A look of understanding crept into his eyes. "Ah, no, I didn't. Look, Anne, I just wanted to know if you might be interested in joining another choir. I found out this morning that I'm short an alto in the chorale that's going to tour Europe this summer and I thought you might want to go."

His request stunned me and my response, when it finally came out, sounded like a ridiculous high school cheer. "Yes," I screamed with delight as I clapped my hands. "Of course I want to go!"

He threw his head back and laughed. "Calm down. Calm down. The trip isn't free. Everyone has to contribute three hundred and fifty dollars, and there's lots of new music you'll have to learn. So maybe you'd like to take a couple of days to think things over."

"No! I don't need a couple of days to think it over. I've dreamed of going to Europe my whole life! I can't even believe you're asking me. This is so fantastic! I don't know where I'll get the money, but I know I'll get it somehow."

"Your family lives in Edina, don't they?" he said as he leaned over and grabbed the stack of music on top of the piano.

"Yes." I answered automatically although I wasn't sure what that had to do with anything.

"So, your parents are rich," he added with a wink as he headed out the door. "They can probably help you out."

• • •

The article *Time* magazine ran in the early 1960's said that Edina, Minnesota was one of the richest suburbs in the United States. If that was true, it was true for everyone but my family.

Returning from World War II a decorated war hero, my father bowed to my mother's demand to "get out of the army" and within one month retired from the active ranks as a Lt. Colonel and joined the Army Reserves.

It was a decision with catastrophic consequences. He was a warrior skilled in battle, not a part-time soldier trained to live in peace.

From that day forward every job he held proved to be only temporary and over the years, he never let my mother forget how much her request had cost him.

Our move from the city of Minneapolis to the suburbs took place during a brief period of prosperity for my father. However, it soon became apparent that moving there was one thing and staying there was another.

To the outside world our custom built five-bedroom home on an acre of land told everyone we were successful. No one would have believed we were poor, although with bill collectors on the phone and at the door, that is exactly what we were.

Swearing me to secrecy, my mother admonished me daily not to say a word about our finances to anyone, and I never did. None of our well-to-do neighbors ever knew that nurse's training served a dual purpose for my parents. My mother could fulfill her prophecy for my life, and it was the cheapest form of advanced schooling they could find.

Even though I didn't think my father had the money I needed for a trip to Europe, I thought he might know of someone who did. He didn't.

When asked, he was abrupt and to the point. "No, I don't know anybody who will loan you the money. In fact, your mother and I aren't in favor of you going at all. You need to finish your training before you go gallivanting all over Europe."

My mother chimed in. "Quite frankly, Anne, I don't think you sing well enough to be a member of a choir that's going to tour Europe. I'm surprised you were even asked."

I didn't react to my mother's painful remark. I never did. The pact that I'd made with myself years earlier still held: I was never going let her see how much her words hurt me. The more she struck out, the more determined I became to hide the pain.

In time, I did find a way to defend myself and it drove her crazy. I simply stared at her. "Don't you give me that look of yours," she'd scream in fury and frustration.

And so, on that day, I sat rigid with practiced calm and stared at her.

"You know, Mother, you're probably right. I don't think I have that great a voice either, but I do pretty well in a choir, and if you won't help me out with this, then I guess I'll just have to find someone who will."

I asked everyone I knew for the money.

Eventually, the assistant director of nurses contacted a generous supporter of the choir and he agreed to give me an interest-free loan on the condition I pay it back within a year of graduation. I was ecstatic.

My mother was enraged. "Who gave it to you?" she demanded when I told her I had the money. "Who!"

I never told her. I didn't tell Bob, either. I decided to let him to believe the if-you're-from-Edina-then-you-must-be-rich myth. In truth, I wanted to believe it myself.

It took weeks of extra rehearsal to prepare the choir for the trip, but by the time June arrived, we were ready. Between the sopranos, altos, tenors and basses there were twenty-eight of us traveling. I was the youngest.

Friends and relatives filled the terminal as we boarded the plane for Europe. Bob's wife Joan was among those waving goodbye. No one really knew why she wasn't going. I'd heard talk, of course.

Some said Bob and Joan didn't really get along and that if it hadn't been for their commitment to the church, they would've divorced long ago. Others said their marriage was fine, but that Joan had been to Europe so many times, she decided to sit this one out.

Either way, I didn't care. The only thing on my mind that summer was having fun. When I heard the gossip about Bob's marriage, my only thought was, *so what? His marriage doesn't have anything to do with me.*

The tour was everything I had dreamed it would be and more. We sang Gregorian chants in the great stone cathedrals in London.

We performed impromptu gospel and popular American music concerts in outdoor restaurants and town squares of Italy, Germany and France. We were on television and written up in local papers.

We won choral contests and were featured performers in the International Music Festival in Wales.

And through it all, there was Bob.

Bob, who, from the minute the plane took off, did something he'd never done before. He noticed me. It started with simple questions. Was I excited about the trip? What cities was I looking forward to visiting?

As the tour progressed, so did his attention. He started to smile at me from the director's podium and wink at me as I left the stage.

Soon his questions became more personal. How were my room accommodations and did I get along with my roommates? What did I do on my free time and with whom did I spend it? At some point, a point I hardly dared acknowledge to myself, I knew I'd become special to him. And I liked it.

Five weeks later when our tour came to its scheduled end in Nice, France, I chose to spend the day alone on the beach. I didn't return until late in the afternoon and as I walked into the hotel lobby Bob fell into step beside me.

"Hey, Anne, you want to take the train to Monte Carlo tonight?"

His invitation shocked me. Bob had always made a great public display of how much he disapproved of smoking and drinking and naturally, I assumed this also included gambling. I didn't answer.

"Not to gamble," he added. "I just want to see what the casinos look like."

I was confused. "Aren't you supposed to be twenty-one?"

He gave me a wink. "Not if all you want to do is look."

Still I hesitated.

"Anne," he said with a shrug. "If you don't want to go just say so, but the next train leaves in forty-five minutes and if we're going to go, we need to be on it."

I couldn't make up my mind. A night in Monte Carlo sounded so exciting and yet . . .

He started to chide me. "So, what do you think? Do you want to take a chance at living dangerously?"

I started to weaken. "Well, do you think we can make it?"

"We can make it if we hurry. Go change and meet me back here."

I caved in. "Don't leave without me!"

I ran past the hotel's ancient gold filigreed elevator and flew up three flights of stairs to my room.

Thirty minutes later, with my hair still damp from the shower, I threw on my white sundress, grabbed my navy blue cardigan, tore out of my room and made a mad dash for the lobby. We took off running as soon as I arrived.

The station turned out to be too close for a cab and too far to walk. We made it with only moments to spare. Bob purchased our second-class tickets, grabbed me by the hand and we jumped onto the train just as the doors closed behind us.

Staggering down the aisle, we collapsed into the first two available seats we could find. "That was fun," I gasped as we both fought to catch our breath.

Bob looked at me and smiled.

"What? What is it? You've got a funny look in your eye. Why are you looking at me like that?"

"I'm looking at you with appreciation and joy, Anne. I happen to think you're beautiful."

For two long years I'd longed for this man to notice me. Just notice me. Now here we were riding a train to Monaco and he was he telling me I was beautiful. My cheeks burned with embarrassment. The palms of my hands were moist with perspiration, but secretly I was thrilled. "Thanks," was all I could think to say.

Bob chuckled. "I tell you I think you're beautiful and all you say is 'thanks?' Anne, you either have tremendous confidence or you truly have no idea how pretty you really are."

I shrugged and smiled, but remained silent. No one in my

life had ever said I was beautiful. I was anything but beautiful. Responsible and reliable? Yes. Beautiful? No. The evening had hardly begun and already I was enchanted.

Forty-five minutes later we stepped off the train into the magic of a Monte Carlo night. We strolled along the cobblestone side streets filled with small quaint shops and ate dinner at an outdoor café with tables covered in red-checkered tablecloths.

After an extravagant dessert of custard-filled crepes topped with caramelized sauce and whipped cream, we wandered over to the expansive marble steps leading to one of Monaco's beautiful casinos. I leaned into Bob, "This is amazing," I whispered, as we entered the casino and walked over thick red carpeting woven into a rich floral tapestry and stared up at the immense chandeliers hanging from the vaulted ceilings. And it was. But, as amazing as the building was, it was the sight of so many elegant-looking people standing around the gaming tables that left me filled with awe. The men, dressed in black tuxedos, wore an air of casual confidence like expensive aftershave, and the women who stood beside them sparkled with sophistication in long evening dresses of fuchsia and aqua, gold, green, and ivory. Envy and longing soon replaced my sense of awe. I didn't want to just look like the women wearing the jewel encrusted evening gowns—I wanted to be them.

Everything happened so fast that at the time I wasn't even aware of it. But years later I knew. I knew in that instant I'd decided to get rid of my old life. I was sick of it. I didn't want it anymore. My life was boring and insignificant compared what I saw before me in Monte Carlo.

I didn't want to go back to Minnesota just to feel sad and overwhelmed all over again. I wanted a whole new life.

"Look at the diamonds that woman at the first table is wearing," I said to Bob, who appeared to be as fascinated as I was. "I feel like such an idiot for wearing this stupid white cotton sundress."

Bob tried to reassure me. "You look fantastic. These women are nothing compared to you."

I made a vain attempt to smile. "I don't think I'll ever feel like these women. I always feel so hopelessly out of place."

He reached for my elbow and guided me from table to table on the casino floor, and it turned out Bob had been right; if you didn't gamble, no one bothered you.

We'd worked our way to the other side of the room and were just about to leave, when three other members from the choir met us at the door and extended an invitation.

They'd rented a car, they said, and were driving back to Nice. Did Bob and I want to ride back with them? If they were surprised to see us together they didn't indicate it and I was so happy with their invitation that it never occurred to me to ask how big the car was.

By the time I realized that in order to make everyone fit in the small green Citroen, I had to practically sit on Bob's lap it was too late to back out. I worked my way into the back seat and oozed my body in close to Bob's.

At first I thought I'd be uncomfortable sitting so close to him, but from the moment I experienced the warmth of his body the only thing I felt was safe. *See,* I thought as my body pressed in close to his, *he really is a giant teddy bear come to life.*

The smell of the sea air rushed through the open car windows and joy, singing, and laughter quickly drenched the star-filled night.

Too soon, I thought as we sped down the cliff-side coastal highway. This night is coming to an end too soon.

Once we were back in Nice the hotel lobby quickly filled up with returning choir members. Everyone was trying to squeeze one more hour out of the night.

Along with many of the other singers, I'd harbored hopes that Bob would tell us that there'd been mistake on the itinerary. I wanted him to hear him say there was one more concert to perform. One more city to visit.

No one, it seemed, wanted the tour to end, but to everyone's dismay, within a few short hours it had done just exactly that.

My mind was in disarray. Real life was about to descend upon me and I knew I didn't want mine anymore.

CHAPTER TWO

Where Do You Think We Can Meet?

The choir arrived back in Minneapolis at five in the morning, and given the early-morning hour, I was surprised to see that a large crowd had gathered in the terminal to welcome us home. I scanned the sea of faces looking for Rick, and was disappointed but not terribly surprised when he wasn't there. We'd only been dating a few weeks before I left for Europe, and even in that short period of time I knew that punctuality was not something he did well. Still, Rick and I had managed to get to an occasional movie before the feature started, and I knew I could count on him to be there for me—eventually.

I resigned myself to waiting and was so intent on trying to find a place to sit that I almost didn't see my mother standing at the edge of the crowd wringing her hands and looking as if she was about to faint. Not that there was anything unusual about her appearance. There wasn't. For longer than I cared to remember, her short, white, tightly permed hair had framed her whiter-than-pale face, a face which turned bright cherry-red when she was agitated.

Nor was there anything unusual about her behavior. By her own admission, she'd been a nail-biter and hand-wringer all her life.

I was obsessed with my mother's hands, but after all the destruction they had caused, how could it be otherwise?

The slightest infraction of childhood behavior could open the flood gates to a reign of terror. Torn or dirty play clothes were enough to send her into a mad frenzy of hitting from which there was no escape. No one in the family was exempt from her hands that moved with the stealth of a serpent and could strike with terrifying speed.

Years later she took up smoking to help her deal with her self-declared "fragile nerves," but for most of my childhood it was hand-wringing and nail-biting that manifested her frustration with daily life. That and food. My mother could cook and eat, and she excelled at both. No, it wasn't her behavior that alarmed me, it was the fact she was there at all.

I crossed my arms and watched her approach. "Hello, Mother." My voice was cold. "I'm surprised to see you here."

"Anne, is that any way to greet your mother?"

The tension was already palpable. Where was Rick, anyway? Why couldn't he have been on time for once?

"Anne, I asked you, is that any way to greet your mother? I got up at four this morning just to make certain you had a ride home from the airport and this is how you show your appreciation?"

"I'm sorry," I said, feeling only slightly apologetic. "But I never even asked you to come. I told you before I left that Rick was going pick me up. Remember?"

I didn't want to ride home with my mother. I could barely tolerate her nervous, critical personality when I wasn't tired. A ride home with her when I was exhausted would be disastrous.

Finally, I saw my six-foot-one-inch blond salvation running through the doors.

I waved my arms. "Rick! Over here!"

My mother stood up straighter and set her jaw. The traditional warning signs of trouble were now in place.

"Anne." Her voice was stern. "Tell me you're not going home with that young man."

I begged her. "Mother, please don't do this." At last Rick was by my side.

"So," he said after giving me a brief kiss on the lips. "How was it?"

Suddenly a fleeting thought, *good thing Dad isn't here to see that one,* shot through my fatigued brain. Even though my father's family had immigrated from Germany years earlier, he still believed in many of the strict European rules that governed family behavior. There would be no demonstration of affection in the home and public displays of affection were singled out as "strictly verboten."

I stepped away from Rick. "The trip was amazing but there's someone here I'd like you to meet." I turned towards my mother. "This—is my mother."

Rick pumped her hand. "Hey, this is great! It's nice to meet you, Mrs. Badendorf."

He looked at me, then at my mother, then back to me again. "Wait a minute, I'm confused."

My mother ignored him. "Yes. Aren't we all? I came because I thought Anne needed a ride home. Apparently, I needn't have bothered." Then she turned and marched out of the terminal.

Rick was still trying to sort everything out. "It would have been all right by me if you had gone home with her. She sure didn't sound too happy about this whole mix-up."

"My mom's never happy. Let's just go get my other bag. It should be off the plane by now."

I glanced around the terminal looking for Bob. I wanted to see him one more time. *Where was he, anyway?* I found him waiting for his luggage with Joan by his side, her arm wrapped tightly through his. Whatever their problems had been, they'd apparently vanished during the five-week separation.

Gone was my sense of exhilaration. Gone were the concerts, the bus rides, and impromptu performances at restaurants across Europe. Gone were the jokes, the fun and the camaraderie.

Dread and despair had taken up residence where joy and happiness had once briefly lived.

"You're home, Anne," I whispered as I climbed into Rick's car. "You're home."

Rick deposited me at my front door and made a mad dash back to his car.

"I'm glad you're back," he yelled out the car window as he turned on the ignition. "I'll call you!"

And then he was gone.

I turned and pushed open the front door and before my bags even hit the floor, I knew there was going to be trouble.

Even the smell of bacon frying and coffee brewing, the very smells I had always associated with the occasional calm morning in my household, couldn't quiet my thundering heart.

Without saying a word, my ten-year-old brother Brian and sixteen-year-old sister Jane climbed over my luggage, pushed open the screen door and eased their way out the door to summer school.

I put out my hand to stop them. "Hey, you guys. Why are you leaving so early?"

They didn't answer me. They didn't even turn around.

My older sister Sherry stood in the dining room stacking education manuals for her new job as teller at our local bank.

"Hi, Sherry," I said tentatively. "I'm back."

She glanced up then turned and reached for her purse.

I walked past her as I made my way into the kitchen. My mother, who gave no indication of my presence, stood at the white enamel stove frying bacon.

My father sat at the breakfast table with his morning paper and a cup of coffee, looking every inch the retired army colonel he was.

He still paid strict attention to his dress and treated his civilian suits much as he had his uniforms in years gone by.

His wool winter gabardine suits and silk-blended summer suits were always cleaned and pressed with knife-like creases in the pants.

Shirt collars, board-like in their appearance from the heavy infusion of starch, appeared stiff around his neck, and his perfectly knotted ties were locked in place with a tie bar that bore the army insignia. With his jet-black hair slicked back and his mustache perfectly groomed, he was by any standard a distinguished-looking man. But it was only when he stood that his six-foot-one-inch frame took on a commanding presence.

He was so absorbed in reading the paper, I wasn't sure he knew I was standing two feet away from him.

"Dad." My voice had already started to tremble. "Are you upset about something?"

The explosion was instantaneous. "You're goddamn right I'm upset about something!"

Startled by his outburst and almost ready to drop from exhaustion, I started to cry. I shouldn't have. My father despised anyone who cried.

I bit the inside of my lower lip in an attempt to stop the flow of tears. "Why are you so upset?"

He got up from the table and threw his paper down on the chair. "Why am I so upset? You want to know why I am so upset?"

I nodded my head.

"I didn't hear you, Anne. I asked you a question and by God I want an answer!"

"Yes," I whispered.

"I still can't hear you!"

"Yes! Yes! Yes!"

"Very good, then, I'll tell you. I am upset because my very own goddamn daughter does not know how to conduct herself properly at an airport."

"I have no idea what you're even talking about!" I was treading on dangerous ground. No one in the family ever raised their voice to my father.

"You know goddamn well what I'm talking about!"

And then my brain did a funny thing. It ran a three-second-movie of my arrival at the airport, and as soon as the film was over I knew what my father had been told.

My mother didn't tell him I'd chosen to ride home with Rick. That was obvious. Nor did she tell him I'd never asked her to come to the airport. He might have understood the confusion. No, she had to have told him about the kiss. Only the kiss had power to inflame my father. The kiss was how she would extract her revenge. "Mother! Turn around! Don't just stand there acting like there's nothing wrong. Tell me what you told him!"

"Anne, you leave your mother out of this," my father cut in. "The only thing she did was get up at four in the morning to pick you up at the airport."

"It was you who sent her home and you who made a goddamn spectacle of yourself with a public display of affection."

"Mother! Did you tell him Rick kissed me at the airport? You told him. Didn't you?" Still my mother said nothing.

I stepped towards her. "That was such a tiny little kiss. It was almost nothing. If you told him I made a spectacle of myself then you're a liar! And you know it! "

Suddenly, before I even had time to react, my father's hand shot out, grabbed me by the elbow, and spun me around. With one quick powerful whack of his open hand he struck me across the face. And with that my body gave way to wracking sobs.

After several moments, my mother turned and scolded my father. "I don't think you should have hit her," she said, wiping her hands on her food-stained flowered apron. "I certainly never intended for things to go that far."

I cradled my aching cheek. I was so confused. What was she talking about? What did she mean by "that far?"

"Mother, you stay out of this," my father said as he returned to his coffee and morning paper. "Something had to be done. She was out of control."

Dazed and defeated, my lip bleeding, I walked back into the dining room and found my sister huddled in a chair with her hands over her ears. She was crying.

Nothing was making any sense. I stared at Sherry and then stared into the empty living room.

When I saw my suitcase sitting near the doorway I decided to go pick it up. "I think I'll go to bed," I said to no one in particular.

My mother's voice came from the kitchen. "Anne, I gave your room to your sister while you were gone. So, if you want to get some sleep you'll have to use the bed in your brother's room."

I was stunned. "You gave away my room? Forever?"

There was no response. Only the sound of my father flipping the pages of the paper filled the air and that simple sound ignited every nerve in my body. I felt like I was on fire.

I stomped up the stairs, threw open the door to my brother's room and collapsed onto the brown cowboy bedspread that covered his smaller-than-twin-size bed. My head throbbed, my face stung, and I couldn't stop crying.

I curled myself into a ball and hugged my knees. "I hate this house," I screamed. "Does anybody know how much I hate this house?"

I rocked. I screamed. I lost track of time. At some point my mother came in and stood over me wringing her hands.

"Anne, if you don't stop right this minute I'm going to call Dr. Hansen and tell him to come over here and give you a shot. And don't think I won't. You need to calm down. I looked out the window and saw his car in the driveway."

I tossed aside the bedspread, sat up and glared at her. "Good! Call him. I want him to come over here and see what you've done to my face!"

A momentary look of terror flashed through her eyes. "On second thought, I think I'll drive you back to school myself."

"Oh, no you don't. You said you were going to call Dr. Hansen and I want him over here. I want to tell him everything that's been going on in this house for years! And don't you think I won't."

"Get up. I'm taking you back to the dorm right now. Your father's right. You are out of control."

I waited until after she'd left the room before I got out of bed. Then I went into the bathroom and looked at myself in the mirror.

My eye was already turning black and blue. My lip was swollen. My cheeks were red and blotchy. My nose was running and my head was pounding.

"Anne! Are you coming?"

I said nothing. I threw cold water on my face and went back to get my suitcase. My mother stood glaring up at me from the bottom of the hardwood staircase.

"Do you have any sunglasses in your purse?" Her voice sounded clinical and detached.

"Yes," I said as I crossed in front of her.

"Put them on. I think you'll feel better."

• • •

Hours later, I awoke to the shrill sound of the phone ringing in the hallway. I pulled myself to the edge of the bed, nursed my swollen lip and listened to the phone echo throughout the empty dormitory floor. I felt awful.

Every muscle in my body ached. I shook my head to try and clear my jumbled thoughts and cleared my throat.

And still the phone kept ringing. Why couldn't the stupid caller just give up? Finally, I dragged myself out of bed.

"Hello," I mumbled into the receiver. I cleared my throat then tried a second greeting that didn't require so much effort. "Yes?"

"Anne?"

"Rick?"

"No, it's Bob. I called your house, but they said you'd gone back to the dorm."

"Oh." I sighed. "What time is it anyway?"

"It's four o'clock."

I gently tapped my black-and-blue eye to see if it had gotten any worse. It hadn't. "Wow, I've been asleep the whole day."

"Anne, what are you doing there? I thought you weren't going back to school until Sunday night."

The phones were directly in front of the elevators and I was awake enough to realize that at any moment the elevator doors might open up and deliver a classmate who'd decided to return early from vacation just as I had done.

No one was due back until Sunday, but you could never be sure. Instinctively, I dropped my head and let my hair fall across my face.

I hesitated. "It's a long story and I'm not sure you'd understand even if I told you."

"Try me. I honestly don't care what you have to say. I just want to hear your voice."

"Well, it's a long story."

"Anne, you just said that and you're beginning to scare me. Just tell me what happened."

"Well . . . My dad got upset."

"Anne." Bob's voice was gentle. "Tell me what happened."

So I told him . . . some of it. I told him how my father had yelled at me, and what my mother had said. I even told him that I'd screamed at her and called her a liar. But that was it. I never told him about my black eye or split lip or that my mother threatened to call the doctor to sedate me. I didn't tell him because I couldn't. I was ashamed of my parents and guilt-ridden over my shame.

I hated my mother's constant, never ending hand-wringing and nail-biting. And I hated the fact she lied or exaggerated almost everything.

When she told my best friend, Beth, that I was thrilled about becoming a nurse, I told Beth, "Don't ever believe anything she says. Fifty percent of what my mother says is exaggerated and the other fifty percent isn't true."

I was ashamed because the dresses she wore were in constant need of repair and almost every skirt she owned had stains. But worst of all, I hated how she smelled.

There were days when she reeked of body odor and I couldn't stand to be near her. But I never told anyone about my feelings of shame that left me filled with rage. Instead, I took the rage, dug a hole in the family-cemetery corner of my heart, and buried it. And with every passing year the cemetery grew.

If pressed, I could only think of one positive thing to say about either one of my parents: my father possessed a sense of style. He could be abusive and never held a job for very long, but at least he knew how to dress. But that was it. The only thing about my parents that didn't leave me full of shame was the fact that my father was a real snappy dresser. No, it was best not to discuss my mother and father with anyone. Ever.

"I can't tell you how sorry I am," Bob said when I had finished.

Unconsciously, I nursed my lip and patted my bruised eye.

"Anne." Bob's voice had dropped to a whisper. "I want to see you again."

"You'll be able to see me at choir practice."

"I'm not talking about choir practice."

"What do you mean?" My mouth felt so dry it was difficult to even swallow.

"I mean I want to see you again. Let me take you to lunch or dinner or anything. I just want to be with you."

Like free flowing mercury from a broken glass thermometer, my thoughts began to skitter. *Why had my father gotten so angry about a casual kiss? My mother knew how violent he could be. Why had she told him? I'm through with them, I thought. I'm never going home again.*

But if I can't go home again, then I'm going to be completely alone and I don't want to be alone. You can't see him, Anne, he's married. But what if he got a divorce? Maybe he could get a divorce.

I didn't know how to answer. I didn't know what to say. I simply couldn't get my thoughts to organize.

"Aren't you going to say anything to me?" Bob sounded hurt.

"I'm not sure what you want me to say."

"Just tell me how you feel about what I've just said."

"I don't think we should be talking like this."

"I miss you." His voice sounded so sad.

Silence pulsated over the telephone wires. "Where do you think we can meet?" I finally asked in a voice that was barely audible.

Chapter Three

God Has Given Me a New Vision

I didn't know how I was going to explain my injured face to Bob, but as it turned out it wasn't necessary. By the following morning he'd left with his wife for Chicago and promised to call when he got back.

Ten days later the evidence of my father's violence had long since disappeared, and I was standing at the fourth floor dorm window staring into the street below. I was waiting for Bob and he was already twenty minutes late. His early morning phone call had left me filled with anticipation and excitement, and I'd spent the entire day reassuring my anxious heart. All I really wanted, I kept telling myself, was a friend. But I knew it was a lie. I didn't need a friend in Bob. I needed a savior.

"Well, look at who's here," exclaimed the dorm director as I made my way across the lobby. "My goodness, Anne, you got down here in a hurry. You didn't even give me a chance to buzz your room!"

Almost every student nurse I knew privately referred to

Mrs. Anderson, our dorm director, as "that mean old Mrs. Anderson," and it was a well deserved title.

Petite and stern looking, she'd spent the last ten years monitoring the behavior of every student nurse in the dorm.

Curfews were strictly enforced: arrive after 10:30 at night during the week or midnight on a weekend, and you were locked out. Traditional Friday and Saturday night date behavior in the lobby was carefully observed. Nothing escaped her watchful eye. Her motto was "Virtue is everything," and we heard it constantly.

"Anne," she said with uncharacteristic enthusiasm. "Bob says he's taking you to lunch! Isn't that a lovely thing to do when he's such a busy man? And would you believe it? He invited me to go along and hear all about the tour. Of course, I'm on duty here at the desk so I can't go, but wasn't that a thoughtful gesture?"

"Yes," I said barely able to contain my laughter. "Yes. It was."

"I'd love to see your pictures," Mrs. Anderson called out as we headed out the door and made our way down the street towards his red Chevy Impala.

I gave Bob a sideward glance. "What would you have done if she had accepted your invitation?"

He opened the car door with a flourish and bowed deeply. "Mademoiselle, your carriage is waiting."

I slid onto the seat. "Come on. I'm serious. What would you have done if she'd said yes?"

Bob closed the door and ran around to the driver's side. "She never would've done that. Duty is her middle name. And you know something? She's going to feel better all day long just because I asked her to lunch.

"Hey, let's not talk about Mrs. Anderson anymore. We've

got terrific weather for a drive and I think we should take advantage of it. I hope you're okay with the top down because I've picked out this out-of-the-way place across the river in Wisconsin."

I took out a short white bandana. "That sounds great. Just give me a minute to tie this around my head. I don't want my hair blowing in my face."

"I love your long hair," Bob said as he watched me try and force the bandana over my thick head of brown hair.

I smiled. "I guess I should have brought a bigger scarf but thanks."

"Thanks," he mocked me. "Again with the thanks." He turned on the ignition and we drove off in laughter under a brilliant blue summer sky.

Conversation flowed easily over lunch. We talked about our favorite cities on tour, the choir, the people we'd met, the concerts and festivals. He never mentioned his wife and I never brought her up.

We'd finished eating and were contemplating the dessert menu when suddenly Bob said, "Let's get out of here and take a walk by the river. There are a couple of things I want to talk to you about."

We made our way out of the historic white clapboard restaurant on the edge of the St. Croix River and walked down a wooded path.

"You sure seem to know your way around a lot of places," I said following Bob's lead.

We hadn't walked very far when we came to a bench situated on a small bluff overlooking the tranquil, tree-lined river.

Bob motioned for me to sit down. "Let's sit. And actually,

Anne, I think I do know my way around pretty well. But then, I'm a little bit older than you are, aren't I?"

"How old are you?"

"I'll be thirty-six in two months."

"You sure don't look thirty-six."

"So you think I'm looking pretty good, huh?"

"Yeah, you look good," I answered, embarrassed by my own boldness.

"How old are you?"

I punched him on the arm. "Oh, come on, you know how old I am."

"No, I don't. I know you're about to start your third year of nursing, but that's about it."

"I'm nineteen. I'll be twenty in November."

"Actually, I thought you were older than that."

His comment annoyed me. "Oh, people are always saying that about me," I shot back. "Everybody thinks that because I'm a student nurse I deal with life and death all the time. The truth is most of my patients are just sick, ulcers and stuff. The really sick ones they give to senior nursing students."

"Okay, okay, so you're just nineteen. Do you think thirty-six is old?"

"No, I don't think it's old!"

"Well, I may have been wrong about your age, but I know I'm not wrong about the string of broken hearts you've left behind."

"You think I've had a lot of boyfriends?"

Bob stretched out his long legs, sat back and folded his hands behind his head. "I don't just think it, I know it."

"Sorry, wrong again," I laughed. "I've only had one real boyfriend and he broke up with me a long time ago."

"Ha! I don't believe that for a second."

"Well, it's the truth." I shrugged my shoulders and once again wondered what it was about my appearance that caused so many people to think I had so much experience with life. My mind drifted with the sound of the water lapping against the rocks on the shoreline, and I found myself remembering a conversation I'd recently had with my sister Sherry.

"Do you think I look old enough to be a nurse?" I'd asked her with great sincerity. "I'm worried my patients won't trust me unless they think I'm old enough."

"Don't be ridiculous. Of course you look old enough. You know as well as I do that you've always looked forty years old even when you were in second grade." Sherry never did have much patience with my questions.

"Hey, come back to me," Bob said as he sat up, leaned forward and put his elbows on his knees. "I want to know what you're thinking."

"About what?"

"About me. This . . . us."

"I like it. I like it a lot. It feels like we're still in some far away place. And being here with you in the warm sunlight makes me feel safe."

"Safe?"

"Yeah . . . safe."

"You don't normally feel safe?"

"Not too much." I cleared my throat and quickly changed the subject. "Why don't you tell me what was on your mind when we left the restaurant?"

"I want to leave Minneapolis."

I was stunned. "Leave Minneapolis? Why would you ever want to leave Minneapolis?"

"Because, I think God has given me a new vision. I know it's probably hard for you to understand, but what I'm doing here is not enough anymore. I want to be a greater witness for God and I think I can do that if I move to Los Angeles. If I could make it in films or play at the Greek Theatre, I would make certain that God received all the glory.

"Well, I've never even heard of the Greek Theatre and I think if you moved from here you'd really be missed."

"Would you miss me?"

I looked down at the ground. "Yeah, I'd miss you."

"If I decided to go, would you go with me?"

I jerked my head upward. "Me? Haven't you forgotten about somebody?"

"Like my wife?"

"Yes. Like your wife."

"My wife has a great job with many, many friends. She's dead-set against moving."

"Well, that doesn't change the fact that you're still married."

"Look, Anne, I've wanted to go to California all my life."

"So, why haven't you gone?"

For several seconds he said nothing. "That's not an easy question to answer."

"Try."

He went on to tell me that at the age of three his mother put him on stage at tent revival meetings and that's really when his singing career began.

"After I gave my life to Christ the only thing I ever wanted was to serve Him." He went on. "But . . . and here's where the real conflict starts . . . my dad was a very successful film distributor. I think my mother would've preferred it if he'd made his living some other way, but I always thought it was terrific. Eventually, it felt like I had to choose one over the other. Either I was going to spend my life in the entertainment business or in the church. In effect, it was like I had to choose my mom over my dad, and I couldn't do it. So in the end I became a singer and entertainer for the church. And that's how it's been for years now. But lately I've had this feeling that God's getting ready to use me in a new and powerful way. I think He's telling me it's time to move to Los Angeles."

"Where are your parents now?"

"My dad's dead, and my mother recently joined my two sisters in Southern California."

"So if you're so unhappy in your marriage and your family's in Los Angeles, why don't you just leave?"

During the whole conversation we seldom looked at each other. He gazed out onto the river and I looked at the ground, the sky, the bench, anywhere but at him. Everything made me uncomfortable. Everything made me feel special.

"Because," he said after several seconds of silence. "I'm not a loner. I've never been a loner. Anne, I know I have no right to ask you this, but do you think you can ever find it in your heart to at least think about California?"

I was so stunned I almost shouted my response. "No! How can you even ask me that?"

"Because I'm married? What would you say if I got divorced?"

"Can we just we move onto something else?"

Bob nodded and smiled. "Sure."

"So, what's the second thing you said you wanted to talk to me about?"

"It's nothing, really."

I tried to recapture the moment. "Oh, don't be like that," I cajoled him. "You said you had a couple of things you wanted to talk to me about, and I want to know what the second one is."

"Well, it seemed like you were getting uncomfortable with the last topic of conversation, and this one isn't going to be much better."

"Tell me anyway."

"I've always wanted a child. Joan and I have tried everything, but nothing's worked. She can't have children and we were turned down by the adoption agency."

"Did you ever find out why?"

"No. I never wanted to know."

"I'm sorry," was all I could think of to say.

For the next several minutes we sat side by side in an awkward silence and listened to the sounds of the river.

By the time I glanced skyward and realized the sun had already begun its afternoon descent, I stood up. "I think we'd better go. Your wife will be wondering where you are."

The awkward silence continued as we made our way back to the car. "My wife never wonders where I am."

We arrived back at the door with Mrs. Anderson standing where we'd left her, in the doorway. She gave us an enthusiastic wave.

Bob threw back his head and laughed. "Anne, who do you think decided to install huge plate-glass windows for doors?"

"I don't know. Mrs. Anderson, I guess. You know, 'the better to see you with, my dear.'" I jumped out of the car.

"I'd like to see you again," Bob said under his breath.

"I'd like that too," I called out and ran up the steps.

Nothing was settled. Everything had begun.

Late the following morning I walked over to the main hospital to pick up my schedule of fall classes. I'd just passed several incoming freshmen pouring out of the door marked Department of Nursing when all of sudden it hit me. I'd made it to my third year. I was officially a senior.

"Yes," I shouted to the sky as I made a mad dash to the dorm. "I've made it!"

I leaped up the dorm steps two at a time, swung open the front door and was about to breeze by Mrs. Anderson when she stood up, leaned across her desk, and whispered something to me. I stopped.

"I'm sorry, Mrs. Anderson, what did you say?"

She kept her hands clasped tightly in front of her waist. "I said you have a visitor." She nodded in the direction of the visitor's lounge and added, "And, quite a handsome one at that."

When I turned, the pain in my chest was so sudden and severe it forced me to gasp. Standing in the middle of the room was my father. I felt caught.

I didn't want to talk to him, but this was a public place and Mrs. Anderson was watching. I forced myself to walk over and greet him.

He stood up. "Is there some place we can talk?"

In public he was so polite, so cordial. Anyone who looked at this well-dressed man would've been shocked to discover the intense storms of violence that lay hidden just below his surface.

I took the chair a few feet away from him. "Here is fine."

He kept his smile, but his air and manner had turned cold. "Fine, have it your way. You always do." He sat down. "I'm here because both your mother and I have agreed that since you were so successful in finding the money to go to Europe, you can find your own money for your last year of training."

I found myself doing battle with the tears that threatened to undo me. "You can't do that," I whispered under my breath. "Tuition's due in four weeks and I'm almost out of money."

"I'm afraid that's where you're wrong, Anne. I can do

exactly that. Now, if you want my opinion, I think you should join the army. They treat their student nurses very well, and you'd be getting a monthly stipend in addition to the cost of your tuition."

I clenched my jaw and hissed through my teeth. "How many times do I have to tell you this? I'm not joining the army! They want two years of your life after graduation, and I'm not going to do that."

My father said nothing. He simply got up, retrieved the navy blue blazer he'd hung on the back of the chair and placed it over his arm.

"Well then, Anne, I guess you're on your own."

He never broke his stride as he walked towards the door and nodded to Mrs. Anderson on his way out.

CHAPTER FOUR

I'm a Baptist

Finding a job turned out to be easy. Student nurses were in high demand at skilled nursing facilities, and there were several within walking distance of the hospital. The work was hard and it took up every free weekend I had, but at least it accomplished my goal: I didn't have to join the army.

After that summer I saw very little of my parents and my relationship with Rick, never strong to begin with, quietly faded away. I thought about Bob constantly. I wanted to be with him, talk with him, and laugh with him. I literally ached to hear his voice. He was the last thing I thought about at night and the first thing I thought about in the morning. But there was nothing I could do except sit, and wait, and hope.

Weeks passed.

Finally one evening in early October as I was about to leave the choir room, Bob stopped me. "Could you stay a minute? I'd like to ask you a question."

His voice sounded so casual and unconcerned that I had

no idea what he was going to say next. "Sure," I said as watched him stack sheet music on top of the piano.

"Can you meet me at my car and go get something to eat?"

I was barely able to contain my excitement. "How can we do that? Your car is parked right out front."

"I'll leave first. You wait for a few minutes then follow me."

"Well, where will I meet you?"

"I'll be around the corner two blocks away from the convenience store."

Too nervous to speak, I nodded and glanced around to see if anyone else might have overheard us. The room was empty.

I was a confirmed Lutheran and had attended church all my life. I believed in what the Bible taught and felt at home in the sanctuary. There was no doubt in my mind that I knew right from wrong. But I was in awe of Bob's talent, charmed by his sense of humor and seduced by his fame. Years later a therapist suggested I might have been looking for a father substitute. If that was true, I wasn't aware of it at the time. I fell in love with Bob when I was nineteen-years-old simply because he was the most exciting thing that had ever happened to my teenage heart.

That Tuesday night when we discovered how easy it was to meet in secret, our lives changed forever. Stealth and secrecy slid its way into our daily lives with terrifying ease and it wasn't long before we became masters of stolen moments and covert meetings.

We met on side streets and in small restaurants. We met late at night in city parks and by the lakes.

If we were in the same room at the same time, we became a study in obvious avoidance.

We acknowledged each other when it was appropriate but for all practical purposes we appeared to be exactly what we'd been telling ourselves: just friends.

Underneath the surface, however, everything had changed. Now every glance held a special meaning, and every love song he sang, Bob sang just for me. He wooed me through his music and won my heart.

I accepted every constraint he imposed on the relationship. We met when he could meet. I never called him. He never called me. All our arrangements were made when we were together. Sometimes I saw him once a week, sometimes only at rehearsal. If I wanted to keep track of what he was doing, all I did was pick up the paper and read the entertainment section. If I wanted to see more of him, all I had to do was find out where he was performing. By January of the following year, I had committed my life to him completely. For him, I wanted to leap into the unknown. For him, I put aside all thoughts of right and wrong. He was the prince of the fairy tale I had written for my life, and I knew he had come to save me.

Sex was never an issue. We never even discussed it. There were occasional stolen kisses, but for reasons I didn't fully understand, sex made me nervous. I craved love, romance and excitement—not sex. And Bob gave me what I craved. The secrecy of our relationship made my life exciting. His constant words of love and adoration filled my heart and my dreams. When he put his arms around me I felt safe, protected and special.

If he felt any guilt about our relationship he didn't show it. The subject of religion came up constantly, but we never discussed the morality of our behavior. After all, what was wrong with being just really good friends?

One clear night in late November we sat on a park bench bundled up in winter jackets, blankets, and each other when the subject of religion, once again, became the topic of our conversation.

"Annie," Bob asked, "are you saved?"

I'd never been asked that question before and assumed that what he really meant was, was I confirmed. "Saved? You mean confirmed?"

"No. Saved. Have you given your life to Christ?"

"Well, sure. That's what you do in the Lutheran church when you go through confirmation classes."

"No, that's not what I mean. When you're a Baptist—"

"Wait a minute. I'm getting all confused. I thought you were a Methodist."

"No, I never said I was a Methodist. I'm only on staff at the Methodist church because they needed a Minister of Music when I was looking for a job. I was born and raised a Baptist, and I believe what the Baptists believe."

"And what's that?"

"That you have to be born again and have a personal relationship with Jesus Christ."

"Well, I have a personal relationship with Jesus. I've had it since I was a little girl, but I'm still a Lutheran."

Bob shook his head. "No. That's not what I mean. You know something, Annie? Sometimes I find myself thinking that maybe God has brought us together just so I could be a witness to you."

I laughed and sprang to my feet. "A witness? A witness for what?"

"Look, I have absolutely no idea what you're talking about and right now I don't want to know. I'm freezing to death and it makes me nervous when you start asking me questions I don't know anything about. It makes me feel like your faith is special and somehow Lutherans just don't measure up. But I know that I love Jesus and Jesus loves me. And that's all there is to it, whether you're Baptist or Lutheran or whatever. Now let's go and get some hot chocolate. Grab the blankets. I'll race you to the car."

Bob didn't move.

"What?" I laughed and tried to pull the blankets from under him. "Come on let's go."

He stood to his feet and wrapped me in his arms. "Sometimes things seem so simple when I'm with you."

"Well, sometimes things really are that simple, so there. Now, can we go? It's cold out here."

"Even in my arms?"

"Yes," I shouted and took off running towards the car. "It's November and only crazy people go to the park in November!"

We built a world around ourselves and thought we had fooled everybody. We were wrong.

I'd never discussed the depth of our relationship with anybody, not even Ilene, my roommate since my freshman year in training. But that didn't mean she hadn't noticed.

"How long do you think you can go on meeting Bob like this?" she asked one night as we sat at our desks studying for our upcoming final in Pediatrics.

"What do you mean?"

"You know what I mean."

"No, I don't. Bob and I are just really good friends."

"Well, you'd better watch it. Other people might not see it the same way."

And she was right.

"Anne, you have a phone call," sang out one of my classmates in the last week of February. "And it's a m-a-a-a-n."

I walked to the phone with an impending sense of doom. If it was Bob, it could only be bad news. Please God, I prayed, please don't let it be Bob. It was.

"Something's happened. I need to talk to you tonight."

"Can't you tell me what it is over the phone?" I tried to keep my voice steady.

"No. I need to see you in person. Meet me in a half an hour at our usual spot."

The lounge was filled with guests when I slipped out the front door, and Mrs. Anderson, for once, was so busy talking to one of the students, she never noticed me leaving.

The clear winter skies made the freezing temperatures easier to bear, but even so, by the time I'd reached his car the cold had seeped through my coat and made its way into my thick sweater. The blast of warm air from the car heater felt like a warm blanket from heaven.

I slid into the car. "You've been crying."

"She knows about us."

"Who knows about us?"

"My wife, that's who!"

"Well, fine. So, what's there to know?"

"Anne!"

My heart refused to hear what he was trying to tell me. "What?"

"You know I'm in love with you—really in love with you. I can't hide it. I don't even want to hide it." He paused. "A friend of Joan's saw us last night at the restaurant. Joan has asked me . . . " His voice faltered. "She's asked me not see you again."

"Please, please, please don't say you said yes."

"I said yes."

His words exploded into my chest like a detonated bomb. Suddenly there wasn't enough air to breathe and I could hear the sound of my own blood pulsating in my ears. I tried not to cry, but I couldn't stop the tears. They were already there.

Bob went on. "What you don't know is that several years ago my wife had an affair. And it wasn't just a one-night stand. It went on for three years.

"I didn't know a thing about it until I came home early from rehearsal one day and found them in bed together."

I didn't know whether to believe him or not. He'd never mentioned this before. Why was he telling me now?

"I can tell by the look on your face that you don't believe me, but it's the truth," he said as his tears spilled down his cheeks. "We should've gotten divorced, but we didn't. We agreed to stay together because of our commitment to the church."

"It's so odd that all of this is happening now."

"Why?"

"Because, I only have one more three month rotation to do and it's in mental health. I'm scheduled leave for Rochester on Monday. You must've forgotten."

When he didn't answer, I knew Bob was going to give his marriage one more chance. Nothing I said would change a thing. I turned and reached for the door handle. "Well, I guess there's really nothing more to say. Is there?"

Bob stretched out his arm to stop me.

"Anne, will you look at me?"

"I can't."

"Why not?"

"Because if I do I'll lose whatever control I have left."

He placed his hand beneath my chin and turned my face toward his. "I need you to look at me."

My tears turned into wracking sobs. "I thought you had come to save me."

"Save you? Save you from what?"

"I don't know! Nothing! Everything!"

He stroked my face and gently kissed me. "I love you, Annie," he whispered as he touched his forehead to mine. "I've waited my whole life to find you."

Then he glanced at the clock on the dashboard and said, "I have to go."

I jerked the car door open.

"Anne! Wait!"

My tears gave way to anger. "What?" I screamed in pain and frustration. "What is it you want from me?"

"I want you to know I really love you."

I jumped out of the car, climbed onto the snow-packed sidewalk, and watched his car drive away until the last fumes from the exhaust pipe disappeared into the cold night air. "Well I really love you too," I cried out to an empty street.

I didn't know what to do. I couldn't even remember how to find the dorm. Worse yet, I didn't care. My dripping nose was becoming a problem and I needed a tissue badly. In desperation I used my woolen mitten to wipe my nose and that only made everything worse. I simply couldn't think. The night air had a numbing effect on my brain.

For several seconds I stood and stared at the frozen icicles under the streetlight and wondered how anything so cold could be so beautiful. Finally, I just started walking.

Several blocks later, after the cold had blanketed my face in stinging nettles and left my fingers and toes throbbing, I realized I was walking in the wrong direction and turned myself around.

"It isn't over. It isn't over. It isn't over," I shouted in cadence with each willful step I took over the hard packed snow. "He'll be back. He'll be back. He'll be back."

Without Bob my life was a black hole of the emptiness. Without Bob I had nobody. Without Bob I felt like I didn't exist. What would I do if he didn't come back to me? How was I going to survive?

• • •

I left Rochester the following Monday convinced that Bob would write. "He'll write." I told my anxious heart. "You know he'll write."

But I was wrong.

Every day at noon throughout the month of February, I ran from the main hospital back to the dorm to check for the mail. And every day at noon the mailbox was empty.

I refused to be defeated. "That's okay," I told myself. "He'll probably call instead."

"I'll get it," I screamed in a frenzy of hopefulness each time the phone rang.

But it was never for me.

Every morning I awoke with renewed hope and the process would repeat itself all over again.

I worked at the hospital and spent time with other student nurses on my days off. I went to church on Sundays and prayed. "Please, God, please. You've got to make my heart stronger. This just hurts too much. "

Every hour of every day it felt like a boulder sat square in the middle of my chest. I had to remind myself to breathe.

"Breathe, Anne, breathe," I told myself. "He'll write. You know he'll write."

But he never did. By mid-March I'd given up on running to the mailbox and soon gave up running to the phone.

Eventually, I stopped talking to the other student nurses and spent all my off-duty time curled up in bed reading romance novels. I'd run out of energy and run out of things to say. When winter's final blizzard blew through Rochester at the end of March, I developed strep throat and was confined to the infirmary.

"You look terrible," the tough old infirmary nurse told me. "You young gals party all weekend long and then come in here sick as dogs on Monday."

I said nothing in my defense. My throat felt too raw. I could barely swallow let alone talk.

One week later I left the infirmary and took the small flame of hope that still flickered in my heart for one more trip back to the mailbox. And still it was empty. This time when I returned to my dorm room, I pulled down the shades and spent the rest of the day in bed. Despair had come to stay.

And then one day towards the end of April as I was walking from the dorm to the main hospital, I made a stunning observation. Flowers had begun to poke their way up through the recently frozen winter ground. Spring was on its way and somehow I'd made it through.

With hope overtaking experience during my final week of rotation I made one last trip to check for mail. I'd barely turned the key when I saw a thin white envelope staring at me from behind the glass door.

I reached in, picked it up, and tenderly tucked the letter addressed in Bob's handwriting behind the bib of my starched white pinafore.

"He loves me," I whispered as I closed the door to my dorm room. "I know he still loves me."

All attempts to open the envelope failed: my hands were trembling too hard. Finally, in desperation I pulled out my bandage scissors from my uniform pocket, cut it open, and took out one flat white sheet of single-lined paper.

My Darling,

In January when I promised my wife I would no longer see you, I felt that in all fairness to her, I should have no further contact with you. She wanted to give our marriage another chance and I agreed.

Yet I find I can't go on like this. I've told her I've never been so miserable. My life means nothing to me if you're not in it.

I'm hoping against hope that you'll see me when you get back to Minneapolis. Do you think there's a California in our future?

Yours, now and always,
Bob

I hugged the pillow and sobbed tears of relief. Saved. I'd been saved. I was going to live after all.

CHAPTER FIVE

When Can We Get Married?

Our reunion took place on the back lawn of the St. Paul Zoo. An obscure spot to meet, I thought, even for Bob, who's knowledge of out-of-the way places was vast. It took me three bus transfers and a twenty-minute walk to get there and still I was early.

After I found a secluded park bench I sat down to look out over the grounds, and to may amazement I discovered that Bob had, in fact, chosen a perfect spot for our reunion. Acres of green velvet grass dotted with small ponds and water fountains covered the landscape. Late-blooming spring tulips filled the flowerbeds surrounding the heavy wrought-iron gates that marked the back entrance to the zoo. It was beautiful. It was so beautiful in fact, I was surprised that there weren't more people there. *It must be the weather,* I thought. It's still chilly for May.

I'd dressed for the cool spring weather in new dark brown linen pants and a matching cable-knit long-sleeved sweater set.

It was the nicest casual outfit I owned. In truth, it was the only nice outfit I owned.

Uniforms, clinical shoes, and school tuition had taken most of my money that year and even though I'd skipped a few meals to stretch my budget, I thought my new outfit had been worth it. New clothes always had a way of making me feel special and I desperately wanted to feel special on this day of celebration.

It wasn't long before I saw Bob's red convertible with the top down pull into the parking lot. I had to smile. Did Bob ever put the top up on his car? I doubted it. Maybe he would in a snowstorm, but that was about it.

With memories of a back eye and split lip lurking in the caverns of my mind, I was determined that I would not make a spectacle of myself. I watched as Bob searched the grounds. "Don't run to him, Anne," I murmured to myself. "Don't run. This is a public place."

Finally he spotted me. "You're here. You're here. You're here," he repeated over and over again as he gathered me in his arms and hugged me so hard that my feet left the ground.

"What's this?" I asked pointing towards the ground where Bob had tossed a brightly colored blanket.

"It's from my alma mater," he said as he picked up the University of Minnesota blanket and spread it out on the grass. "I thought we might need it today."

I grabbed the sodas I'd purchased on the way over and we settled in.

"Have you noticed anything different about me?" Bob asked in between dozens of light, feather kisses he continually planted on my face and neck.

I stared at him with admiration and pride. "You've lost weight."

"I've been going to the gym five days a week and eating only one meal a day."

"Do you think that's healthy?"

"Never felt better. I'm going to keep going, too."

"Well, just so you know, you don't have to lose weight for my sake, okay?"

He leaned over and kissed me again. "Annie, you make me feel so blessed."

For the next hour and a half we basked in the warmth of the sunlight we'd convinced ourselves had come out just for us and the intense feeling of safety that always surrounded me when we were together returned. Nothing, I thought, could ever diminish the glow of this afternoon. Once again I was wrong.

"Annie," Bob said minutes before he had to leave.

My body tensed. "The way you said that frightens me."

"No, come on. I need your support in this."

"In what?"

He dropped his gaze to the ground. "I'm not going to be able to file for divorce right away."

"But, I thought you'd done that already!"

"What are you taking about?"

"You said in your letter that you'd told Joan that you were miserable."

"I did tell her."

"So, I thought that meant you'd gone ahead and filed for divorce."

"Divorce is not that simple, and you know it." He sounded annoyed. "Joan told me yesterday that in order to get the divorce, she's going to have to charge me with mental and emotional cruelty."

"Oh, nobody ever believes that stuff."

"Maybe. Maybe not. But when people find out I'm getting a divorce, they're going to stop calling me for work and my income is going to drop. If they think I abused my wife, it may stop all together."

I simply couldn't understand why he was so concerned. It was inconceivable to me that he would ever be anything but a success. In concert after concert I'd seen how the public adored him. "I think you're making way too much of this," I told him. "No one's ever going to believe that you abused your wife. Everybody's going to know that's just something you had to say to get a divorce. Besides, people will hire you because you're talented and you're the best man for the job—not because you're married or divorced or whatever."

The truth of the matter was this: I knew nothing about Bob's world or the fundamental teachings of his church and even less about divorce. I was worse than naïve. I was ignorant and scared. I didn't want to hear about any more obstacles. Obstacles frightened me. The only thing I wanted was the safety of marriage, and from that day forward I would minimize or ignore any potential problem that threatened my hoped-for future. Bob made my life complete. Without him I simply didn't exist.

"If only that were true," Bob said caressing my face. "I want this to work out as much as you do. It's just going to take time. The important thing is that Joan knows how I feel, and that you and I are together."

I bit into my lower lip in an attempt to hold back the tears. "How long do you think it will be before you file for divorce?"

"I'm not sure. I pray about this all the time and God will tell me when the time is right. You do want God's blessing, don't you?"

I nodded.

"Well, then, we'll just have to wait. God will tell me when the time is right." There was nothing I could do but wait.

That summer I graduated from training, passed state boards, took a position working nights at the University Med Center in the Intensive Care Unit, and found a tiny one-bedroom apartment. Small as it was, the apartment gave us something we'd never had before: freedom.

No more Mrs. Anderson. No more secret meetings on side streets. No more self-imposed phone restrictions. Now we were free to talk to each other any time we wanted. Now we were free to hold one another in each other's arms without fear of being seen. And now, we were free to make plans for our future together in California.

Sex, however, was still off limits.

"Anne, do you find me physically attractive?" Bob asked late one afternoon after we'd eaten lunch and he was preparing to leave.

The question surprised me. We'd never even mentioned our sexual attraction to each other, let alone discussed it.

"Of course, I do. I melt inside every time I hear you sing and my heart bursts with pride whenever I hear the audience applaud. Besides, you're funny and you make me laugh."

His eye twinkled. "I am pretty good. Aren't I?"

"You're more that good. You're amazing."

"Well, if that's how you feel, why don't you show me?"

"Because we're not married and you're still living with your wife."

"I've told you I'm going to file." His voice was full of exasperation.

"I know that. But when?"

"Annie, please . . . "

"No, I want to know when. You said you were going to file when the time is right. Well, I want to know. Is there ever going to be a right time?"

"I don't know. I keep praying about it, but it just seems to get harder and harder. Joan said I could stay in the house through Christmas. That's one good thing about having such a big house. She can live in her half and I can live in mine."

"And then you'll file?"

"Sort of."

"What does that mean?"

"It means that Joan and I have agreed to let her do the filing. She thinks it will allow her to save face."

I had no idea what saving face meant and was too afraid to ask. I wanted him divorced. What did saving face have to do with anything? "So, she's going to wait until after Christmas and then she's going to file?"

"Yes. Annie, you don't look very happy."

"It's just that Christmas seems so far away."

He looked sad, but his words were filled with anger. "You have no idea how much I'm giving up for you, do you?"

His voice frightened me and his words confused me. Wasn't he the one who'd said he wanted to go to California with me by his side? I stared at him. I didn't know what to say. I didn't know what to think anymore. Overnight my apartment, which had initially been so freeing, had become a prison. My world had begun to shrink with alarming speed and the day Bob asked me to be very selective about any new friendships I made, my world got smaller still. I went to work. I went to church. I saw Bob. That was it.

"Well, I'm out of time," he said as he reached for his keys. "I'd better get going."

"Please—please don't leave like this. I don't like it when you're upset with me. I love you."

"I know you do, Annie. But sometimes I wish you understood things about my life better. You don't understand the stress I'm under. You don't understand how much creditability I'll be losing in the church. And now in addition to everything, our relationship is beginning to feel like my marriage. You seem to lack any kind of passion for me and . . . "

"That's not it at all!"

"Well, what is it then? What!"

"I'll tell you. Just don't leave me, okay? Put your keys down, and then I'll tell you."

He put his keys back in his pocket and waited.

"I'm holding back, because—I feel so stupid telling you this—because my mother always said 'Don't expect any man to marry you if you have sex with him before marriage. No matter what he promises. In the end, every man wants the woman he marries to be a virgin.' And, as silly as it sounds, I think she's right."

Bob's face softened. "I wasn't asking you to have sex. Well—" He paused before giving me the slightest glimmer of a smile, "at least not right now. I just need something more."

"Like what?"

"Like maybe a lingering kiss with a slightly more passionate embrace thrown in."

"That's all? Really?" I breathed out a sigh of relief and wrapped my arms around him. I'd just have to work on being more patient. If that's what it took, then that's what I'd have to do.

CHAPTER SIX

You've Dishonored the Family

When Joan finally filed for divorce the following January, I was happy and relieved, and so was Bob . . . sort of. Consumed with his public image, as always, he quickly put together a new set of rules to govern our emerging relationship, and rule number one was that under no circumstances were we to give the public the impression that we were a couple . . . ever. I could attend his performances, but all conversations were to take place in private. Holding hands was out of the question. As disappointing as the rules were, I didn't find them surprising. What was surprising was this: overnight the word marriage simply vanished from our conversations. He never mentioned it again. I told myself that all he needed was time, but when time didn't help, the terrible possibility that he might have changed his mind began to haunt me. The thought alone terrified me, but the fact that it might actually be true made me literally sick to my stomach. For two years, Bob's love for me and his promise of marriage was all I had lived for.

What was going to happen to me if we didn't get married? A whispering campaign of nameless faces began to obsessively chatter in my head. "Oh, didn't I tell you about her? Poor thing. She threw her life away on a married man." Every week the pressure built and every week my obsessing got worse. Months passed and still I said nothing. Finally on a seemingly ordinary Sunday evening in late fall I exploded.

It had been our custom to watch television each Sunday evening before I reported for duty on the night shift at the hospital and that particular Sunday evening was no exception.

The empty take-out cartons from our recently consumed Chinese dinner still littered the coffee table when Bob abruptly decided to get up and turn on the television set. In that instant something inside my head and heart exploded. "Turn it off. We need to talk." My words sliced through the air.

He hesitated.

I got up and stood next to the television. "I said turn it off."

An odd look of confusion crept into his eyes, but he did as he was told.

"I want to know what your intentions are."

He sat down on the sofa. "What do you mean?"

"I mean do you ever intend to marry me?"

"Annie, you know I love you."

"I'm not talking about that! I want to know if you ever intend to marry me!"

Bob walked over to sofa and sat down. "Come here," he said as he patted the cushion.

"No! I don't want to. I want an answer."

"The answer is yes, I intend to marry you."

"When?"

He reached out for my hand.

I ignored his gesture and leaned against the kitchen counter with my arms crossed.

"Look, I thought your divorce was going to take a few months. It's taken almost a year. All we do is talk and this may come as a big surprise to you, but I'm sick of it. We've talked in parks. We've talked in out-of-the-way restaurants. We've talked in small little towns I've never even heard of before. We talk and we talk and we talk. I've done everything you've asked of me. You told me I had to be patient. Well, I've been patient. You told me we couldn't be seen in public alone together and I went along with that. You told me you were afraid people were going to stop calling you for jobs. Some have and you've lost some big jobs, but a lot haven't. You told me you had to leave the church you were in and find another church. Well, you've done that. Maybe it isn't as grand as the one you were in, but it's still pretty big. I want to start living that life you promised instead of sitting around talking about it all the time. I want to get married and move to California. We can do this, I know we can. In two months your divorce is going to be final, so what are we waiting for?"

Bob's eyes filled with tears and his chin quivered. "You honestly think everything is going to work out, don't you?" I walked over and sat down next to him on the sofa. "Yes, I do. What is wrong with you, anyway?"

"I'm scared, Annie. I've wanted to do this my whole life and now I'm just plain scared."

"You're going to be successful. You know you are, and even if we do struggle a little in the beginning, so what? I can work until you get established."

"You'd do that for me?" Bob looked surprised.

"Sure, I would. I mean I don't want to do it for my whole life, but we can always use it as a back up."

"You really believe we can make this thing work?"

"There's not a doubt in my mind."

He stared at me for several seconds and then pulled me onto his lap. Finally, he spoke the words I'd waited three years to hear. "Well, if you honestly think it can work then I think we should just do it. If we get married this summer, we can take a trip to Los Angeles for our honeymoon and look for a place to live at the same time."

I searched his eyes for reassurance. "You're not just saying this because I'm upset?"

"No. I really mean it." He smiled for the first time that evening. "Now, wrap your arms around me because even though I know I love you more than life itself, this whole thing terrifies me."

I was ecstatic. It was all going to come true! I ignored the fact that Bob told me he was terrified.

I ignored the fact that after we'd chosen a wedding date he became so busy I seldom saw him.

I ignored the fact that he had no interest in planning the wedding. "Just do what you what you want, Annie," was his answer to everything. I ignored it all.

The one thing I couldn't ignore was telling my parents. I didn't know if they knew about Bob or not, but I knew where they stood on the subject of divorce. They hated it. I dreaded making the phone call.

"Mother, this is Anne."

"Well, so it is. I was beginning to think you had completely forgotten you had parents."

"No. I haven't forgotten. Listen, the reason I'm calling is I need to tell you something before . . . "

"I have no idea what this is about," she cut in. "But it

sounds like something you should be telling your father as well."

"No! You can tell him everything when we're done. Mother, do you remember Bob Mansfield, my choir director at nursing school?"

"The one who asked you to go to Europe? Of course I remember him. In fact, you know I recently heard the most awful thing about him. I heard he left his wife, that poor thing. And they'd been married such a long time, too. It's such a shame when things like that happen. Everyone says she's such a lovely woman and never did one thing to deserve it. I wonder what possesses people sometimes. Well, what about him? I certainly hope he's not asking you to take another tour is he? Now that you've just gotten the other one paid off. You did pay off your loan, didn't you?"

The pressure in my chest built with every word she spoke and soon a rivulet of sweat began making its downward journey from my temple onto my neck.

"Yes, Mother, I paid it off a long time ago. And no he hasn't asked me to take another tour."

"Good. Not that I think you have anything to worry about. After all, he's practically old enough to be your father. Still you can't be too careful."

"Mother, will you stop talking for one second please!"

"Anne, there's no need to be rude."

"I'm sorry. It's just that I've called to tell something. I've called to tell you I've been seeing Bob since his divorce."

"Seeing Bob? What do you mean by seeing Bob?"

"Seeing, Mother, as in dating."

"You can't mean that. I know people have said they've seen him with a girl young enough to be his daughter, but never in a million years did I think that was you! Anne, please tell me you would never do such a thing, especially when you know how your father and I feel about divorce."

"No, I'm not going to tell you any such thing. I only called you now because I didn't want you to hear it from somebody else."

"Where are calling from?"

"My apartment. Why?"

"Because your father and I are coming over right this minute and talk some sense into you."

"No! I don't want you to come! We can talk about it over the phone."

"No, we can't. We are going to have a nice, calm, reasonable discussion on why you have decided to throw your life away."

"Please, mother. Let's meet somewhere . . ." But she'd already hung up.

I had to find Bob. I called the backstage number Bob had given me for the symphony rehearsal hall and reached the stage manager, but he was adamant in his refusal. It would have to be a life-threatening emergency before he'd pull Bob out of rehearsal. He would, however, give him a message that I called. By the time Bob returned my phone call fifteen minutes later I was hysterical.

"Annie, what's wrong? The stage manager said you were upset."

The words rushed out of me. "You've got to come over here right away. All I did was tell my mother we were dating and she flipped out. I didn't even get a chance to tell her we've started to plan the wedding. She's on her way over here right now with my father!"

"Sweetheart, calm down. I can't come right this minute, but I'll be there the second rehearsal is over."

"But I need you to come now! My mother and father are already on their way."

"I know you're upset, Annie, but they're your parents. They're not going to do anything to hurt you. Just keep remembering how much we've been through and how much I love you. Listen, I have to go. I'll be there as soon as I can."

I hung up the phone. "I've got to get out of here," I whispered as I frantically searched for my car keys. I found them just as I heard a knock at the door. I froze. *Don't move.* I thought. *Maybe they'll just go away.*

"Anne," my mother's voice sounded so kind. "Please answer the door. We saw your car on the street, so we know you're home."

Her voice sounded so kind, in fact, that I actually thought for one moment maybe this isn't going to be so bad after all. I opened the door and they brushed by me.

"Where on earth did you get this furniture?" was my mother's one and only question.

I was well aware that everything in my apartment was mismatched and the rose-colored sofa clearly clashed with the apple-green carpeting. But still I was filled with tremendous pride of ownership and fiercely defended my choices. "The Salvation Army. Their store matched my budget."

"It looks awful and it's really much too big for this apartment."

"Look, Mother," my father cut in, "I don't give a good goddamn about her furniture and neither do you. Anne, I'm going to get straight to the point. Your mother tells me that you are dating a fat, old, divorced man. Now, before I go and get all upset about this, I want to know is this true?"

"Yes, except he isn't fat and he isn't old." *Don't cry, Anne. Whatever you do don't cry.*

My father's right eyebrow arched and he drew the corner of his upper lip into a cynical sneer. "That is all a matter of opinion now, isn't it? What I have to say to you, Anne, is this. You are to end this relationship as of here and now. Is that clear?"

"Yes." I forced myself to look at him.

"Good, I'm glad we have that understood. Does that mean you'll do it?"

"No."

My father eyes exploded with a burning fury. "You have brought shame on our entire family and I won't allow it! If you don't end this relationship, I'm going to demand you leave this city."

"I'm not a child anymore! I'm twenty-two years old and you can't tell me what to do!"

"Anne, listen to your father," my mother admonished me. "We can't stand idly by while you continue to dishonor the family name. We're going to send you to San Francisco to stay with your father's cousin, Caroline. She's agreed to help with anything you need until you get settled."

"I won't go! I've never even met Caroline. Besides, everybody in this family has somebody but me. All I've ever been is good old responsible reliable dependable Anne. Well guess what? Now I have somebody who loves me and we're going to get married. "

My father's response was immediate and swift. He grabbed me by the wrist and threw me across the room.

Whether he had intended to slam my head into the wall or not did not matter. I ended up dazed on the floor. Through a distorted haze I could see my mother wringing her dry, chapped hands, and over the ringing in my ears I could still hear my father's voice.

"We're buying you a plane ticket and you're going be on that plane two weeks from today, because I'm going to personally see to it that you are. And don't even think of running away because I'll find you. No daughter of mine is going to throw her life away. I won't allow it."

I struggled to get off the floor and noticed a small stream of blood trickling down my hand. My father's fingernails had gouged the skin loose. I picked off the skin and began rubbing my head. "I hate you," I said through clenched teeth.

"Say what you want," my father said. "But two weeks from today you're going to be on that plane, and someday you're going to thank me for saving your life."

"I want you to leave," I said. Nobody moved. "Are you deaf? I want you out of here!" And still no one moved. "Well, fine, stay if you want, but the next person you're going to see coming through that door is Bob. He's on his way over here right now."

With that, my father opened the door and pulled my mother into the hallway. "You have two weeks left."

I was running cold water from the faucet at the kitchen sink over my bleeding hand when Bob walked through the door fifteen minutes later.

He stroked my hair as I told him what happened.

"Maybe," he said as he put pressure on my hand with a paper towel, "maybe it's not such a bad idea."

"How can you even say such a thing?" My voice cracked.

"Listen to me. It'll give us a chance to prove to everyone that our love for each other is really strong. This might be God's way of testing us."

"Oh, you're always telling me what you think God is trying to do and I'm sick of it! I don't need any more tests."

"Sweetheart, you're just upset. You need to try and see this from God's point of view and look at what He is asking us to do. He's asking us to honor your parents and if we do, then He will honor us and bless our marriage."

I pulled away. "And just how long do I have to stay away in order to pass this test?"

"I can't tell you that. Only God can."

The more Bob talked, the more frantic I felt. "I don't think God has anything to do with this. I think you're trying to get rid of me. I don't think you want to marry me."

Bob reached out and cradled me in his arms. "Nothing could be further from the truth. I only want what's right in God's eyes. Remember, Anne, it's your parents that are asking you to do this."

I pulled out of his embrace. "Why is everybody trying to send me away?"

"Annie, please. If you go to San Francisco, if only for a little while, by the time you come back they'll know there's nothing they can do to stop us from getting married. We can get through this. You just have to be strong."

My thoughts were all so jumbled. Why wasn't Bob fighting for me? Could my parents actually force me to leave the city? But what was the point of staying if what Bob said was true? Maybe this really was a test from God.

I searched Bob's face in vain looking for a reprieve. "I don't want to be strong anymore," I sobbed. "I don't want to be patient anymore. I don't want to be anything anymore except married."

Once again Bob gathered me into his arms and kissed my hair. "Annie, please do this for me," he whispered.

Two weeks later my father, looking dapper as always, picked me up at my apartment. "Where's mother?" was the only question I asked him on the thirty-minute drive to the airport.

"She's at home." He kept his eyes on the road. "You're doing the right thing, Anne. I know you're going to make us proud of you."

"When we get to the airport I want you to drop me off. Don't help me with my luggage and don't walk me into the terminal to see if I get on the plane."

There was nothing more to say. I didn't care if they were proud of me or not. The only thing that mattered to me was Bob. And Bob wasn't there.

Caroline met me at the airport with a placard bearing my name and her kindness and generosity helped ease the pain of my banishment. When I accepted the night position in the orthopedic wing of San Francisco General two weeks later, it was Caroline who helped me move into a women's residence in the city.

As soon as I checked in, I rushed to a pay phone in the hallway and put in a collect call to Bob. He wasn't home.

Disappointed and disheartened, I returned to my room to put away the few things I'd brought with me. The room was small and spare.

The bed was narrow and covered with a plain light-brown chenille bedspread. The dresser might have been maple, but it was so old and scratched it was hard to tell.

The multi-colored braided rag rugs were like the ones I'd remembered from my grandmother's farmhouse in northern Minnesota. The whole atmosphere depressed me. It was as if the gray fog of the San Francisco Bay had seeped in through the window and permeated everything I touched. I would've wished for a nicer place, but that was impossible. In one of those sad ironies that seemed to plague my life, neither my parents nor Bob offered me any financial help in making the transition to San Francisco. The money I'd brought with me was just enough to pay first and last month's rent, and hopefully get me through until my first paycheck.

I'd just finished unpacking and was in the process of sliding my suitcase under the bed when I heard a knock at the door. The noise startled me.

The trance-like world in which I now lived didn't allow for loud knocks at the door. I walked over and opened it.

"Hi," two girls said in unison.

"I'm Judy," one said.

"I'm Agnes," added the other.

"I'm Anne."

"Yes, we know," said Judy. "We checked with the front desk to find out who our new neighbor was. Would you like to go get some tea or something?"

"Are you from England?"

"Indeed, we are," Judy chirped. "Did our accents give us away?"

I smiled for the first time in weeks. "Yes, they did. Where are you from?"

"London," they chorused again. "And," Agnes added, "we are working our way around the world and having a jolly good time doing it, aren't we Judy?"

Judy nodded her head yes. "Right you are, Agnes. So what do you say, Anne? Do you want to go get some tea with us? It's almost four o'clock. You're going to need something to hold you over 'til supper."

"Umm . . . thank you so much, but I'm waiting for a phone call. Maybe next time?"

"Oh, a phone call is it? Must be from a man," Judy said

with a wink. "That's the only thing anyone would wait for around here. Well, maybe next time then. Ta!"

I closed the door, eased myself onto the bed and looked around the room. Isolated, alone and desperate, I felt like a stranger, even to myself. Where was Bob anyway?

Every hour on the hour I called him and just when I thought I would collapse into total despair, he answered the phone.

"Where have you been?" I sobbed. "I've been calling you all night."

"Annie, calm down. I was at rehearsal and some of us went out to get something to eat afterwards."

"Oh, I thought maybe you'd given up your apartment and gone back to Joan."

"That's so crazy. In the first place she wouldn't have me, and in the second place I'm in love with you."

"You are?"

"Yes. I am. I miss you—how are you?"

"Terrible. Really awful. I start orientation for my new job tomorrow, but I don't think I can do this. I can't even figure out why I'm here. Why did I come here, anyway? Just to make my mother and father happy? Is that why I'm doing this?"

"We're doing this to prove to them how strong our love really is. And, we want God to bless our relationship."

"Won't God bless us anyway? I mean, we love each other. Isn't that enough? I'm so confused about everything and I miss you so much. My parents don't want me to come back to Minneapolis, ever. You know that, don't you?"

"But you are coming back. Both you and I know that."

"Why can't I come back now?"

"Annie, give it at least a couple of months."

"I think I miss you more than you miss me."

"I love you and I miss you. I'm sorry you're having such a hard time, but things will get easier. I know they will."

"How do you know?"

"Because I'm praying for you."

My voice dropped to a whisper. "I don't think you're prayers are working. I'm feeling ashamed of what we've done. That's the real reason I'm here, isn't it? I'm being punished for dating a married man."

"Annie, don't be ridiculous. You're there because we're being tested. God wants to see how strong our love really is. You're going to be fine. We're going to be fine. I'm going to keep praying and you'll see. God's going to honor our love for one another."

I wasn't sure that Bob had everything figured out when it came to God, but I seldom disagreed with him. I needed to believe his prayers could work. I needed to believe that God could make things easier for me because He was listening to Bob's prayers. But more than anything I needed to believe in Bob.

"Annie?"

"What?"

"My prayers are going to be answered. You'll see."

I asked if we could set up a regular time to talk.

"I don't think that's going to work," he replied. "Between your schedule, my schedule, the three hour time difference, and the pay phone, it's going to be pretty rough."

"Well, shall I just try and call you when I think you're going to be home?"

"Let's not set anything definite. You call me or I'll call you."

"Okay, but remember I'm only on days for a week, then I go to nights."

"Then you'd better get some sleep. I love you."

"I love you, too."

I hung up the phone and walked back the long dark corridor to my room. "How," I wondered as I lay my pounding head down on the bed, "am I ever going to get through this?"

I made it through one week on nights and then started to unravel.

At the start of second week I walked into staffing office and requested a transfer, but there weren't any openings. At the end of a month I decided orthopedic nursing held little interest for me and again I asked for a transfer. But just as before there weren't any openings.

I called Bob constantly. It didn't make any difference to me if he was home or not. If he was home I was thrilled. If he wasn't, I had the next call to look forward to. I took the bus to work every night and watched San Francisco's city life through a rapid transit window. Friendships were impossible. How could I make new friends when I went to bed just as everyone else getting up? I joined a choir in a large downtown church, but found the people to be as cold and foggy as the weather. I bit my nails until they bled. I ate little and slept less. Four months later on the edge of emotional collapse, I decided to return home.

When I informed my parents, they said I would regret it forever. When I told Bob, he said we had passed God's final test. I chose to believe Bob.

Once back in Minneapolis I moved in with two staff nurses from the University Medical Center and returned to my old job in the Intensive Care Unit. Bob and I immediately reset our wedding date for July and though he wasn't thrilled about being involved in the arrangements for the actual event, neither did he ignore me as he had done in the past. He did have one request.

"Keep it small, Annie. Just keep it small."

My father was so disappointed by my decision to return home that he stopped talking to me. If he had something to say to me, he said it through my mother.

"Anne, your father has said that if you insist on marrying that man, there will be absolutely no financial help whatsoever," or she would say, "Don't expect your father to walk you down the aisle. He says he won't do it."

Then again, "I hope you don't intend to embarrass the family any further by wearing white. After all, this is the second wedding for Bob. Your father and I haven't decided whether we're coming or not. But, if we do, we have no intention of being part of a three-ring circus, so for God's sake keep it small and don't wear white."

My mother's obsession with the wedding festered and grew daily. She was against my plan to marry Bob and was on the phone constantly. If she failed to reach me at home to complain, she'd stay on the phone until she reached a friend or relative. She called my roommates, my aunts, uncles, neighbors, my grandparents, and my sisters. And each day the list of people she called grew. She called the pastor of the church I grew up in and the pastor of the church I presently attended. No one could escape her cry of "Why is Anne doing this to us?" And no one could give her a satisfactory answer.

Soon relatives and neighbors, many of whom thought I was destroying my family, began calling, and with every phone call the determination I'd developed and nurtured through endless days and nights of desperation in San Francisco began to erode.

Tremendous interest had developed in my every move and my mind soon jumped back onto the roller coaster of doubt and confusion.

Was I, in fact, making a huge mistake? I decided I needed an outsider's opinion.

I needed someone who had no vested interest in whether I married Bob or not. *Someone,* I thought, *who could help me sort things out.*

I chose the head psychiatrist of the mental health unit where I'd I trained. He was fascinating and insightful in the classroom, but sadly for me, cold and distant in the office. When I asked him, "Do you think marrying Bob is the right thing to do?" he rocked back on the edge of his swivel chair, tapped the tips of his fingers together, and responded in a detached, clinical manner, "What I think isn't important. You're wasting your time and money if you came here today expecting me to tell you what to do."

His abruptness startled me and shattered the fond image I'd carried of him since my days as a nursing student. My voice fell to a whisper. "Well, I'm not sure about what I should do. I've been having bad dreams. Not nightmares—just bad dreams."

"About?"

"About living in a concentration camp and there's all this fighting going on.

"That sort of makes sense don't you think?"

"In what way?" I asked, more confused than ever.

"Well, there's a tremendous amount of upheaval going on in your family right now."

"So that's why you think I'm dreaming about concentration camps and war?"

"Could be . . .Tell me, Anne. Are you afraid of anything in particular?"

Instantly, I went on alert. Did he already sense something about my father? "What do mean by afraid? Afraid of what?"

"Oh, I don't know . . . flowers, animals."

"Flowers?" I asked in disbelief.

"Yes. Or animals."

"Well, I don't like Birds of Paradise. I think they're ugly."

"Uh, huh. Birds of Paradise. That's very interesting."

His questions and responses astounded me. "Look, unless you can tell me what Birds of Paradise have to do with whether or not I should marry Bob, I feel like we're just wasting each other's time."

He said nothing.

"I'll give a check to your secretary."

I got up from my chair, walked out of the building and made my way to the bus stop. "What an idiot," I said to myself as I boarded the bus. The strength of my resolve had returned. Now nothing—not phone calls from concerned relatives, not an obsessive mother, nor a disappointed father who no longer talked to me was going stop me from marrying Bob. He was my reason for living.

In truth, he was all I had.

CHAPTER SEVEN

Do You Honestly Think You're a Christian?

Four years after it all began, Bob and I were married on July 1, 1964. The wedding dress was simple to please my mother. The ceremony was small to please Bob. My father refused to give me away. My mother advised me, "don't even ask him." And I didn't. It was not a happy event.

The afternoon wedding took place in the chapel of the Lutheran church where Bob served as the new Minister of Music. I was so grateful to my older sister Sherry when she agreed to sit at the main table and pour coffee for our cake and punch reception, I never pressed her to have her picture taken with me. I did, however, ask my brother, Brian and my parents. When they all declined, any hope I harbored of having a normal reception vanished. And through it all I smiled.

I smiled when I told Bob my family refused to be photographed with me. I smiled when he laughed and said, "I guess that means you'll have more pictures taken with me, then!"

I smiled when he said to his friends—many of whom I

was meeting for the first time—"I want you to meet my Annie. She's my wife!" His joy was so obvious it almost took my pain away.

I smiled even though many of the guests seemed to sense my family's discomfort and left the reception almost as soon as it began. And I smiled when the Senior Pastor came to me at the end of the reception and asked, "Anne, what are you going to do with the wedding presents that were left on the table?"

"Oh." I felt my throat tighten. "I'd arranged for one of my roommates to take them home. I guess there must have been a misunderstanding. I don't know what to do now."

"Can you take them in your car?"

My mind drew a blank and still I continued to smile. "Well . . . maybe." Bob arrived from the men's room just as my smile muscles were about to collapse. "Oh, that's easy," he said. "Let's just put the gifts in my office."

A few minutes later the church janitor, a slight, white-haired man whose kindly spirit shone through his clear blue eyes, shuffled his way to the door and waved us off.

I started to sob as soon as the car pulled away from the curb. "It wasn't supposed to be like this," I cried as I pulled out a tissue from the glove compartment.

Bob looked surprised and concerned. "Annie, what are you talking about?"

"I mean it wasn't supposed to be like this! I hated my dress. I hated my parent's sullen faces. I hated the reception. It was just a bunch of people standing around eating cake and drinking punch. It wasn't a party at all! And why wouldn't anyone have their picture taken with me? "

Bob tousled my hair. "Do you hate me?"

"No, don't be silly. Of course I don't hate you. I love you. But—"

"Well, that's good," he said as he turned the car onto the freeway heading south. "Because as of right now you are my wife and we are starting our new life together. I don't want you to be sad. From now on it's California here we come!"

I was startled by the direction we were taking. "Hey, wait a minute. Why are we going south? Don't we need to be going west if we're going to take the shortest route to Los Angeles?"

"Not if we're going to the dog races first!"

"What are you talking about? I thought we were going to have a romantic wedding night in Minneapolis!"

"Annie, Annie, Annie. There are going to be lots of romantic nights ahead of us, but first we're going to go to the dog races in South Sioux City!"

"But that's in Iowa!"

"So?"

"Well, I've just never pictured myself in Iowa on my honeymoon. Besides, I've never heard of anybody spending the first night of their honeymoon trying to make it to the dog races, whether they're in Iowa or not."

"You're making way too much out of this. Remember what we said when we took our wedding vows? We promised to love, honor, and have nothing but fun on our wedding trip. Now forget about the dog races for a second, and let's talk about where you'd like to spend our wedding night."

If going to the dog races surprised me, the fact that he hadn't made reservations for our wedding night stunned me. "You mean we don't have a place to stay tonight?"

"Nah, but don't worry. There'll be lots of places available."

"Are you sure?"

Bob's voice was full of confidence and cheer. "I've traveled all over Europe. I think I'll be able to find us a place in Iowa. Trust me. I can do this."

I couldn't bear any more disappointments on my wedding day. "I do trust you," I said as I moved closer to him and attempted to force all my doubts and sadness away. "But just in case, I'll help you look for a vacancy sign."

"That's my girl!"

We'd been driving through the flat southern Minnesota farmlands for almost two hours before we crossed the border into the resort area of northern Iowa and I spotted a sign. "There! Right there! Let's take that one! It says they have a pool, color TV, a king-size bed and everything!"

"Sounds good to me."

As soon as Bob said 'sounds good to me,' my heart started to pound. This was it. I was a married woman now.

The nightgown I'd purchased several weeks earlier lay packed in tissue paper in my suitcase.

I was excited, nervous and scared as we walked into the motel office.

The desk clerk greeted us. "May I help you?"

"Yes, you may," Bob said with an affected German accent. "Would it be possible to get a room for myself and my wife?"

I erupted into a fit of giggles.

The clerk looked at Bob, then at me, then back to Bob again. "You are married, aren't you?" he asked rather skeptically.

Again Bob answered in accented German, "Yes, we are." And with that I broke into peels of laugher.

"Annie," Bob said, now laughing, "what is going on with you?"

The clerk handed him the motel key.

"I don't know. I guess . . . I guess it feels so weird to hear you call me your wife. Especially with that German accent!"

"Congratulations," the clerk yelled as we made our way back to the car.

Once we'd collected the luggage and placed it inside the room, Bob took me by the hand and led me out into the hallway. "You know what I want to do? I want to start all over again and do this right."

"You're crazy," I shrieked as he swooped down and carried me over the threshold. Enveloped in laughter, we tumbled onto the bed.

"I want to show you the nightgown I bought for tonight," I said, wrapped in his embrace.

Bob was busy planting feather-like kisses on my neck and face. "And just how would you like to do this?"

"Well, I thought I would just slip into the bathroom and change."

"What an excellent idea and while you're doing that, I'll wait for you in bed."

I jumped off the bed, gently lifted the nightgown out of my suitcase and made way to the bathroom. "I'm going to need a couple of minutes to get ready," I said closing the bathroom door.

I loved the pale pink nightgown I'd purchased for my wedding night. The floor length sheer silk fabric in the skirt was attached to the bodice with satin piping, and the lace neckline plunged into a deep v-cut. "Do you think this too low?" I'd asked the salesgirl in the lingerie department. "Not if it's for your wedding night," she answered with a knowing smile.

As I stared at myself in the motel bathroom mirror, I concluded that it had been worth every penny I'd paid for it. I loved the way the soft fabric draped over my body and caressed my skin. It made me feel beautiful.

And now the anticipation was over. The approving gaze I'd imagined a hundred times on my bridegroom's face was only seconds away.

"What's taking you so long?" Bob yelled from the next room just as I'd finished my preparations.

I turned off the bathroom light and opened the door to a darkened room. "Hey, wait a minute," I said as my eyes tried to adjust. "I wanted you to see me. Why are all the lights off?"

"Forget about the lights." Bob was still in a playful mood. "Just come over here and get into bed with me. I've been waiting for this night for too long."

Disheartened and confused I stumbled my way across the room. "I still want to show you my nightgown," I pleaded.

"I know you do and I want to see it, but just slip out of it for now and get into bed."

The moment was gone. I did as I was told. "I don't understand why you turned out all the lights."

"Because," Bob said as he reached for me, "you're so young and beautiful that next to you I feel old and ugly. I'm not ready to have you see me yet. I just want to make love to you."

A wave of compassion swept over me as he encircled me in his arms and my body began to respond to his kisses.

"I've never felt beautiful—not ever. All I wanted was for you to see me in my nightgown. I wanted it to be like in all the books I've read where they say things like, 'He gazed at her with wonder.' "

"In the morning," he whispered, as his lovemaking became more urgent. "In the morning."

He was a gentle if disappointing lover. No bells rang. No

rockets went off. Long after he'd gone to sleep, I was still awake.

I listened to his breathing as it became deeper and deeper. "It wasn't supposed to be like this," I murmured as I reached down to the floor and slipped the nightgown over my head.

I awoke the next morning to Bob's smiling face and continued good cheer.

"Annie, come on. We've got to get going. It's later than I thought and we've got to hustle. I don't want to be late for the races." Bob leaped out of bed and ran towards the shower.

I didn't even know we were late much less that we'd overslept. "What are we going to do about breakfast?"

"We'll grab something on the road," he shouted back through the closed bathroom door. "We don't have time for anything else."

Within a matter of minutes we were dressed, packed, and out the door. The subject of my nightgown never came up again.

"You know, I'm still not quite sure what to make of this whole dog race thing," I said once we were on the road. "It feels awfully weird. What does the Bible say about it?"

"About what?"

"About gambling!"

"I've never found any place in the Bible that states 'Thou shalt not go to the dog races.'"

"Fine, make fun of me it you want, but I still think it's very odd that you know so much about gambling. First it was Monte Carlo and now this."

"Well, when we win a lot of money you just might not think it's so odd!" We arrived at the races with plenty of time to spare, paid our entrance fee at a small wooden ticket booth, and walked through gate.

The ticket-taker was a craggy-faced old man dressed in blue jeans, a faded denim shirt and a sweat-stained, cream-colored Stetson. "Hope you guys win big today," he said with a big smile that revealed his tobacco-stained teeth.

I smiled back and glanced up at the stadium that lay just in front of us. Everything looked so ordinary.

The covered aluminum bleachers built to one side of the racetrack looked exactly like the bleachers I remembered from my high school football games. The vendors calling out, "Peanuts! Popcorn! Ice cold drinks! Get your ice cold drinks here," to the already assembled crowd made everything appear so normal that it now seemed as if my upset was a terrible overreaction. "Maybe, this isn't going to be so bad after all," I yelled at Bob who'd rushed ahead of me towards the stands. The air alone seemed to intoxicate him. I shook my head in disbelief as I watched him study the dog-racing program with the same intensity I'd seen him study a musical score.

"Here," he said pointing to a name in the program. "I think I've found a winner. I'm going to the betting window. You stay here."

He returned with sodas in hand wearing a big smile.

"See, didn't I tell you this would be fun!"

I rolled my eyes and smiled. I still couldn't believe we were at the dog races on my honeymoon, but Bob's happiness was all that mattered to me. And there was little doubt that Bob was happy at the dog races.

Suddenly Bob was on his feet. "Annie, look at our dog! He's in the starting gates! Come on, Runs-Like-the-Wind! You can do it!"

From that point on Bob jumped, yelled and screamed

throughout that race and several more to come, but it was all to no avail. We lost every single race.

When we finally won on our very last chance of the day, Bob threw his hands up in the air and shouted, "Thanks be to God! We've won a lot of money!"

But his excitement quickly vanished when he looked at the scoreboard and realized our windfall consisted of exactly sixteen dollars and thirty-eight cents. Apparently, we weren't the only ones in the stands who thought the dog was going to come in a winner that day.

Disappointed but not discouraged, we returned to our car and headed back to the interstate. At last, we were on our way to California.

Over the next three days, the panorama of the United States passed before my eyes. The rolling cornfields of Iowa gave way to the flat wheat fields of Nebraska. The wheat fields of Nebraska soon turned into the wide-open ranges of Wyoming and Wyoming brought us into Utah, and with every passing mile my sense of security grew. Minneapolis, and all that had happened to me there, faded further and further into the distance. And then came Salt Lake City.

The day we crossed over into Utah the entire state, including Salt Lake City, was in the middle of a sweltering heat wave. We'd already agreed that we wanted to be in Las Vegas by nightfall, and because I knew little about the Mormon religion and absolutely nothing about the Mormon Temple, I saw no reason to stop.

But Bob said he wanted to drive into the city and see the Temple, and if Bob wanted to see it, that was reason enough for me.

When they told us we weren't actually going to be allowed inside the Temple we were disappointed, but even in the heat the gardens that surrounded the Cathedral were spectacular.

We'd just completed our tour when Bob suggested we return to the car and pray.

I felt a trickle of sweat run down my neck and back. "Pray? Now? In this heat?"

"Yes, now, in this heat. Let's get in the car. I want to look for a certain scripture verse. This will only take a minute."

We returned to the car, which in the short time we'd been away had already turned into an oven, and Bob reached into the glove compartment to retrieve his Bible. I brushed back the hair that was sticking to my face and neck and watched as he searched for the scripture verse he wanted. "Here it is. Proverbs Chapter three: verses five and six. Trust in the Lord with all your heart. And lean not onto your own understanding. In all your ways acknowledge Him and He will direct your path." When he finished Bob had tears in his eyes.

"Annie, we should have never dated while I was married. What we did was wrong. We've hurt Joan and broken one of God's commandments. We need to ask for God's forgiveness for the pain we caused and turn back to Him for His leading."

The sweat dripping from my forehead began sending warning signals that a migraine in the distance was moving closer. I had to get out of this heat.

I knew we shouldn't have dated while Bob was married, but we had covered this ground so many times before. I tried to humor him. "Can't we just pray and get back on the road? At least that way we can get some air circulating. I swear this is the last car we're getting without air conditioning. Convertible or not."

He ignored my attempt at humor. "Just tell me something will you? Do you honestly think you're a Christian?"

"What's gotten into you, anyway? You're scaring me. We've been over and over this. Every time you've asked me if I'm a Christian the answer has always been the same: yes."

"But I still don't think you understand what I mean. What I want to know is, are you born again? Do you truly accept the Lord Jesus Christ as your personal Savior? Do you have a personal and intimate relationship with Him? Do you know He died for your sins? Do you know that if you were the only person on earth, He would have died for you and you alone? Because that what's I believe and I want to know if you believe it as well."

"Look, we're both sitting here sweating, my head is pounding, the air is stifling and you want to know if I truly believe in Jesus."

"Well, do you?"

"Yes! I told you before my answer was yes. And it's still yes. Nothing's changed since then. I'm sorry we hurt Joan. I think about that a lot and it always makes me feel really bad, but I thought if we didn't have sex that somehow we weren't doing anything wrong. Besides, you said you loved me. You said you'd been waiting for someone like me all your life. You said you never thought you'd love anyone as much as you loved me—and I believed you."

"I do love you." His voice had softened, but his eyes still burned. "Annie, did it ever occur to you that maybe God intended to bring us together so that I could be a witness to you?"

"Here we go with that witness thing again. Every time you talk about being a witness it doesn't make any sense to me. Why are you so intense about this? You look like a crazy person." Tears mingled with sweat now oozed down my face.

"I don't mean to frighten you. All I meant to say was

maybe God is going to use me to help you understand what it means to believe in Jesus Christ."

"Does this mean you don't love me anymore?"

"I love you more than life itself . . . Annie?"

"What?"

"You don't understand what I'm talking about, do you?"

"In a way I do and in a way I don't. You know I believe in Jesus. I just don't understand why you're making such a big deal about it right now. What I really need to know is do you love me?"

"I love you."

I breathed a sigh of relief. "Good. That's all that matters to me."

He reached for my hand. "Pray with me. We need God's forgiveness so that we are able to receive His blessing."

I did as I was told but I was confused.

Bob had assured me that if I honored my parents' request and moved to San Francisco, we'd have God's blessing. I thought we'd already passed the final test. Why was he now telling me something else?

After he finished praying, he put the Bible back in the glove compartment and gave me a quick kiss. "Okay, that's it. The next stop is Las Vegas and I sure hope you love it as much as I do!"

Through tears and sweat I gave Bob an automatic smile. Everything suddenly felt wrong. I longed to go back to being normal again, but I knew that wasn't going to happen. Nothing in my life had been normal for years. Normal was what happened to other people, not me.

Chapter Eight

Trust Me

In the distance the bright lights of Las Vegas danced across the evening sky. "Is that it?" I asked barely able to contain my excitement. "Is that Las Vegas?"

"That's it, Annie!" Bob's voice echoed my own enthusiasm.

"This is amazing! It almost looks like an enchanted city. Where do you think we should stay?"

"Oh, who cares! Nobody ever goes to bed in Las Vegas."

My stomach tightened. "But we're going to find a place to stay, right?"

"Why don't we just wait and see how we feel."

I slumped down in my seat. "Oh, Bob please."

My reaction confused him. "Trust me, Annie, Las Vegas is going to be more fun than anything you've ever imagined. The last thing anyone wants to do in this town is sleep!"

"Okay. But promise me if I get tired we'll get a room. I hate being tired. Once I get tired, I'm a wreck. I get nauseated. I feel like I'm going to throw up. My head starts hurting . . ."

"Fine." Bob laughed. "If you get really tired, we'll get a

room. Now, look out the window, will you? We're about to drive down the famous Las Vegas Strip!"

All around me neon lights flashed, darted and jumped around giant screens shouting out names of the visiting celebrities, hotels and anything special the hotels had to offer. CHEAP FOOD! BEAUTIFUL SHOWGIRLS! TOPLESS DANCERS! There seemed to be something for everybody in a city where excess was the norm.

I stared at the names on a hotel marquis. "Do you think those people are actually here?"

"What people?"

"Those people," I said pointing to the names of Frank Sinatra, Sammy Davis Jr., Dean Martin. "Do you think they're all here?"

Bob's eyes glistened. "Of course they're all here. That's what's so great about Vegas."

My excitement mounted by the second. "Do we get to see someone perform?"

"I doubt it. The shows are really expensive."

As quickly as it had built, my excitement disappeared. I felt my shoulders sag. "Oh."

"Oh, come on, Annie, don't look so glum. We're going to have a terrific time. We'll go see the lounge acts and you're going to be really surprised when you see how good they are. And Annie?"

"What?"

"Trust me."

"Oh, you always say that. It's like you think you always know better and you don't want to hear anything more from me."

Bob reached over and tousled my hair. "You'll see."

"And quit messing up my hair!"

After several minutes we found a parking space and headed off down the Las Vegas Strip.

"Where would you like to begin?" Bob asked as put his arm around me and hugged me close to his body.

I resisted his attempt to cheer me. "Why are you asking me? You're the one who knows Las Vegas." Then suddenly I saw a sign that brought me to a dead stop. "I can't believe this," I cried out. "I cannot believe this!"

"Believe what?"

"Look at that marquis over there! It says Debbie Reynolds is here!"

"So?"

"I love Debbie Reynolds! I've loved her ever since she did *Tammy and the Bachelor.* Can't we please go see her? Please? I won't ask you for another thing for as long as I live if we can just do this. I promise."

"Annie, you know we need to save as much money as we can for the move. Frank Sinatra's here and we're not going to see him—and you know how much I love Frank Sinatra."

I forced myself to smile. "I guess you're right."

Once again Bob wrapped his arm around my shoulder. "Hey, I've got an idea. Let's walk over to the hotel where Debbie Reynolds is performing and take a look around. Maybe she'll come walking through the lobby."

"Okay." I tried to sound enthusiastic, but even I knew that his suggestion was a pretty poor substitute for seeing Debbie Reynolds in person.

And then we walked in the hotel lobby. It was breathtaking. The sheer size alone was staggering. Spectacular fresh cut flower arrangements stood on marble tables. Heavy burgundy and gold tapestry carpeting covered the lobby floor that led down to the steps of the casino. Ornate chairs and benches upholstered in matching brocade print were scattered everywhere. Several people walking through the lobby were dressed in evening clothes, and a few of the men even wore tuxedoes. But as breathtaking as it all was, the glamour of Las Vegas couldn't compare to what we'd seen in Monte Carlo. Here, I didn't feel so out-of-place in my light green summer cotton dress.

The air was heavy with the scent of perfume and the smell of smoke. "Cigars must be a really big deal when you come to gamble, huh?" I asked as we walked down the steps from the hotel lobby onto the casino floor. But Bob didn't hear me. His eyes already held the slot machines in laser-like focus. I followed his gaze around the room.

Everything was a peculiar blend of the strange, wonderful and bizarre.

People of all ages sat at the slot machines dressed in everything from simple khaki shorts to elegant evening clothes. Shouts of joy or cries of despair could be heard as large sums of money were being won or lost at the roulette wheel. Exotic looking women strolled through the crowd in sequined cocktail dresses that displayed their ample cleavage and sometimes more.

Bob grabbed me by the hand as we worked our way through the crowd to the teller's window.

"What's that noise?" I shouted. "What's all that clanging?"

"That's the sound of money! The slot machines are paying off. Now if you'll just follow me, young lady I'm going to show you how it's done."

"How do you know about all this stuff?"

"I'm older than you are, remember," was his only answer.

He exchanged twenty dollars for several rolls of quarters and nickels and then turned to me. "Quarters or nickels? You pick."

"Nickels! I don't want anything more. I'm scared I'll lose everything."

The energy of the room was contagious and it wasn't long before I was consumed with delight when the clanging of the one-arm-bandit began to sing its jackpot song for me.

The hours flew by. We played the slots, ate, laughed, and consumed gallons of Diet Pepsi. We hit every hotel along the strip, listened to the ever-changing lounge acts and somehow managed to stay ahead of our losses.

Finally, at 4:00 A.M. just when I wanted to call it quits, Bob decided he was going to try his hand at blackjack.

"I want to find a table that calls my name," he said scanning the room.

Once he'd made his decision he slid onto a high stool across from the dealer. I watched him play out several hands before I urged him to call it a night.

But my words fell on deaf ears. "Can't you wait just a little bit longer?" he asked slightly annoyed. "I want to try and win back some of the money I've lost."

"How much have you lost? I'm so tired I haven't been paying any attention."

"Not much, but I'd still like to come away feeling like a winner. Why don't you sit in the lobby and people watch for awhile?"

The excitement of the evening was gone. The thrill of seeing a celebrity or watching Bob play twenty-one wasn't nearly as appealing as crawling into a bed.

"Bob, you promised." I knew I was whining but I was passed the point of caring.

"Annie, please. Just for a little while longer. Who knows if we'll ever be in Las Vegas again."

The dealer stared at me with his arms folded across his chest. The table became very quiet.

I caved in. "Okay. I'll go find a chair in the lobby." Laughter erupted from the table as I walked away and I knew Bob wasn't going to be along any time soon.

My eyes burned from too little sleep and too much smoke. I spotted a black leather chair in the corner of the lobby and fell asleep the moment I sank into the overstuffed cushions.

I awoke with a start. Someone's hand was on my knee.

"Annie, wake up! I won us a lot of money and we need to celebrate!"

"How much money is a lot of money?" I managed a smile even though every joint in my body felt stiff and sore.

"Almost a hundred bucks!"

"Really? That's great! What time is it, anyway?"

"It's seven o'clock. I thought we'd have breakfast and just head out for Los Angeles."

"Are you sure you're awake enough to drive?"

"Are you kidding? I feel great! I have a beautiful young wife and tons of money in my pocket. I feel like I'm on top of the world."

"Where are we going to shower and stuff?"

"We can do that at my mother's."

"Your mother's?" I stood and stretched out my aching muscles. "I thought we were only going to meet your mother in L.A., not stay with her."

"Don't look so worried. My mother's going to move in

with my sister for the three weeks. We're going to have the place all to ourselves."

"I know what you're going to say next so don't even bother."

"And, what might that be?"

I caressed his scruffy face. "Trust me."

"Now you've got it!"

Bob's energy amazed me. As we drove out of Las Vegas, my fatigue was so intense I was nauseous, but he never complained of being tired. Not once.

I yawned and rubbed my irritated eyes. "Don't you ever get tired?" I asked as we passed the Los Angeles city limits sign.

"I'm fanatical about sleep."

"When? When are you fanatical? I've never seen you get tired. Not once on this whole trip."

"Lack of sleep is the first thing that shows up in a singer's voice. If I have to sing, I always make certain I get at least eight hours the night before. Now, do me a favor. Reach in the glove compartment and pull out the map of Los Angeles. It's right underneath the Bible. And get the Bible while you're at it. As soon as we look at the map, we need to give thanks for God's many blessings to us on this trip."

I hated feeling confused and I was getting more confused every day. It was clear to me that Bob was devoted to the words in the Bible, but I still didn't understand how he knew so much about gambling. His love affair with Las Vegas left me bewildered. It bothered me to think that he might be capable of rationalizing his faith to justify his lifestyle, but the evidence was mounting. When he wanted to spend time in Las

Vegas, he'd say "but I'm only having fun." When he wanted to go to Monte Carlo, he'd say "just to look."

And though he'd appeared to be genuinely repentant for his past behavior as we sat in the car and prayed in Salt Lake City, I was beginning to wonder if he'd repented only because he wanted God to bless his new life. On some level, as exhausted as I was, I began to suspect that Bob's faith was the faith of a demanding child.

He wanted everything and in return he was prepared to give almost nothing. But these thoughts drifted through my head like tourists in a foreign land. Nothing took up permanent residence.

As we drove along the San Bernardino freeway on our way into Los Angeles, the only thing that mattered to me was that Bob and I were in love. All the vague thoughts I had, all feelings of doubts and uneasiness, I buried. It was a coping skill I'd developed through years of childhood abuse and it was still something I did very well.

I reached into the glove compartment for the map and pulled out the Bible. "I'm not good at reading these things."

'Well, just do the best you can. We're on the 10 freeway going west and I'm pretty sure we want to cross over to the 405 going north. Can you see where that is?"

My brain refused to work. I stared at the map. The lines all ran together. "Why don't you just call your Mom and ask for directions?"

"If I do that it'll ruin the surprise!"

"Wait a minute! I'm not ready to meet you mother looking like this! I'm exhausted and I feel awful. I need a shower. I want to wash my hair."

"Oh, come on, Annie, I swear to you she won't mind."

"I mind! Please call her and get directions."

"Let's just try this first."

And I did try. But, within a half an hour it was clear to me that we had taken a wrong turn.

"We're lost!" Bob shouted.

I studied the map for any clue that might tell us where we were, but it was hopeless.

"Come on, Annie. Look at the map and figure out where we are."

It was no use. "Look. I told you I didn't know how to read a map and I meant it. I've never had any reason to read a map in my life. Why should I be any good at it?"

"Because everybody knows how to read a map, that's why."

My chin started to quiver. "I don't understand why you're so angry with me."

"You really don't understand why I'm angry with you?"

I cleared my throat. "No."

"Well, try this. I haven't seen my seventy-five-year-old widowed mother in over a year and all I wanted to do was see her face light up. I wanted to bring a little added joy to her life, but now I can't because you've ruined the surprise. You're a smart girl, and maps aren't that hard to read. I think you did this on purpose."

His remark had found its target. I yelled in anger and surprise.

"Why would I ever do something like getting us lost on purpose? You're making no sense whatsoever. Just find a phone booth and call your mother. We're both tired."

Bob pulled into a nearby gas station, yanked the map out of my hands and got out of the car. "I can't believe you don't know how to read a map."

He returned with the map neatly folded and notes scribbled in the margins. "She's going to go over to my sister's now." He still sounded angry. "You won't have to meet anyone until tomorrow night at dinner. I hope you're happy."

I picked up the Bible in my lap. "What do you want me to do with this?"

"Just put it back."

It was a difficult day. Bob remained steadfast in his belief that I had ruined his surprise and spent the rest of the afternoon and evening pouting. We were in bed by nine o'clock. "It wasn't supposed to be like this," I whispered as I watched the sleeping chest of my husband rise and fall.

The following morning Bob led us in devotions as though the map incident had never occurred. He never apologized for his behavior and I never brought it up. But my stomach knew something had happened. My stomach felt like I'd eaten stones for breakfast.

The first call came mid-morning and for the next hour the phone rang constantly. His sisters called. Where should we meet for dinner? What kind of food did I like? How was the trip? Did we bring any pictures of the wedding? His mother called. Was he tired? How did he sleep? How was he feeling? Was the bed in her apartment comfortable? Everyone was very excited about our arrival.

Eventually, it was decided that everyone would meet in Hollywood at the Farmer's Market on Third and Fairfax, and by mid-morning we were back on the 405 freeway heading out for a day of sightseeing.

"Annie," Bob said with a heavy Italian accent as we pulled into traffic. "I'm a gonna show you everything today. First we're gonna go to the famous Chinese Theater. Then we're gonna go over to the famous Paramount Studios and take a little tour. And then, we're gonna have lunch at the famous Nic's Restaurant and after that we're gonna head down to the famous Malibu beach before we head back to the Farmer's Market."

"You forgot to say famous."

"Whadda ya mean, I forgot to say famous?"

"You forgot to say the famous Farmer's Market."

"Well, maybe I didn't forget," Bob said with a twinkle in his eye. "Maybe everything else is much more famous than this Farmer's Market."

He was teasing me. My stomach relaxed. "I love you, you know."

"Well, that's good. Because I love you too."

"I have a really important question to ask you."

"Ask me anything you want and I will tell you the answer."

"Do you know how to find where we're going today?"

"Hey, young lady. You think I don't know my way around? Why, I love this city. And if I can't find my way around with a map and the directions my sisters gave me over the phone, then I just better learn in a hurry. We get lost? Nothing to it," he said with a snap of his fingers. "I call one of my sisters and she gonna tell me what to do. I love my family. And just you wait young lady. You're gonna love them, too."

I felt my stomach relax. Everything was going to be fine. The old Bob was back.

The Hollywood Farmer's market we came to at the end of the day was unlike any farmer's market I'd ever seen. Back home farmers sold seasonal fruits and vegetables in simple white clapboard stands by the side of the road. This market was huge and built right next door to the CBS television parking lot. The market itself was housed in three separate white buildings and contained everything from small boutique gift shops and open-air restaurants to stands filled with vegetables, pastries, seafood and meat. Bob and I got there in time to wander through the shops and browse the restaurant stalls. The menus outside the Thai and sushi restaurants listed dishes that I couldn't even read, let alone pronounce. Everything sounded strange and exotic. Nothing sounded familiar. When the smell of barbecued ribs and chicken came wafting through the late warm summer afternoon air, I secretly hoped Bob would say, "Let's just get a hamburger." But we settled for chow mein from the crowded Chinese counter. It was a happy compromise. Bob loved Chinese food and it fell into the "safe" risk category for me.

We'd purchased our food and were just about to sit at an empty table in the open-air food court when I heard someone yell, "There he is!" And suddenly, Bob's entire family descended upon us, and for the next three hours, his mother, sisters, brothers-in-law, nieces and nephews rained happy chaos down upon our heads.

Quite unexpectedly, I'd found myself in the middle of unanticipated joy and I loved it. *Had I,* I wondered, *finally found the family I'd always longed for?*

Our wedding trip flew by. It took us only three weeks to find an apartment in Sherman Oaks, one of the nicer towns in the San Fernando Valley, and give the superintendent a deposit. Bob continued to meet with several of the contacts he'd had in the music and movie business, but unfortunately no one offered him a job. He wasn't worried, he said. He thought he had charmed them all.

No one said they thought forty was too old for a move to Hollywood. No one said they thought his size and age would limit him to character roles and that the character actors in Hollywood had been there for years.

No one said that choral music was a dying art, not only in the record business, but everywhere else as well. And no one said to him that Ray Coniff, Norman Luboff, and Johnny Mann—three of the biggest names in choral music for the recording industry—had just released their last albums and it was only a matter of time before they dropped from the music scene altogether. No one told him that Los Angeles and New York were the only markets that mattered to anyone.

No one said if you move to L.A. you'll have to start all over again . . . at the bottom. And no one said that churches, even in Los Angeles, would never hire an unknown divorced Minister of Music.

We returned to Minneapolis firmly believing that God was in our corner and our future looked bright. We were completely ignorant of the truth as Hollywood saw it.

The people of Minneapolis never thought Bob would actually leave, but by the time we'd hired a moving company, the obligatory round of farewell luncheons and parties had already begun. The festive atmosphere culminated when the *Minneapolis Star and Tribune* took the entire front page of the entertainment section to list his accomplishments and contributions.

I didn't feel any need to say goodbye to my family. That had been done long ago. And there weren't any friends with whom I needed to stay in touch.

The very nature of my relationship with Bob had required intense secrecy and isolation for so long that I'd lost all my friends along the way. The friendships I so desperately needed, I was convinced, lay waiting for me in California.

There was nothing left for me to do on the morning the moving van pulled away from our apartment except get in the car and leave. I left in tears.

Bob was mystified. "Why are you crying?"

"I don't know. Scared I guess. It feels weird. I've wanted to leave Minneapolis for so long and now all of sudden I'm just sad. We are making the right decision, aren't we?"

"Annie, trust me. We're making the right decision."

CHAPTER NINE

A Baby Will Fix Everything

By the end of our first month in California we'd settled into our new apartment and I'd completed my first week of orientation at the local community hospital. Convinced we'd saved more than enough money to get started, we both saw my working as only a precautionary measure. In just a few short weeks Bob's initial concern over making the move to California had turned into full and complete confidence in himself. "Two—three months tops and something big will come along," was the answer he gave to anyone who asked how long he thought it would take to get started in Hollywood.

But he was wrong. Within weeks of our arrival, rejection appeared at our doorstep and delivered an almost near-fatal blow. No one returned Bob's phone calls. The contacts he'd made only two months earlier were suddenly unavailable. No matter how many times he called, the response was always the same. "I'm sorry he's not in. Would you care to leave a message?"

Soon, an awful reality began seeping its way into my consciousness: Bob had no idea how to get started. In Minneapolis, everyone called him.

He never called them. I'd never heard him make one phone call for an audition or work. Not ever. Rejection was something that happened to others, not him.

With his contacts dwindling, Bob decided to go back to the church and find work as a part-time Minister of Music. But in the sixties most churches weren't hiring a divorced man from another state with a wife seventeen years younger than himself. Even I, naïve as I was, understood the real meaning behind, "I'm sorry, it's against church policy to hire someone who's divorced at this time."

By the end of three months the unthinkable happened: the money we'd saved had evaporated. I watched as my world collapsed with astonishing speed.

I pleaded with Bob. "Please, please let's go back. Nothing is making sense out here. Everything just feels stupid. Nobody knows your work. They don't return your phone calls. We were happy in Minneapolis. We can be happy again. I know we can. You tried it out here and it just didn't work. That's all."

"We're staying," he insisted. "I won't go home as a failure. Everyone says 'if you have talent you'll succeed.' I'm not giving up."

But overnight he did just that.

One day he simply decided that God wasn't going to bless our move to Los Angeles after all and promptly traded our devotional time for the television set.

In the morning he watched game shows. In the afternoon he watched soap operas. And all day long he cried.

My apprehension grew by the day, the hour, the minute until ultimately, it turned breathing into a major event.

The only thing I knew how to do for myself was pray. For me, my prayer life was logical and life saving. I still needed and wanted God's help even if Bob said He had forgotten about us.

I never told Bob I'd developed my own prayer time. Even though my vague uneasiness about Bob's confusing belief system had continued to grow, it was one thing to have my own prayer life and quite another to challenge Bob on his. And none of my uneasiness ever changed my overwhelming need for Bob to be happy and successful.

"Bob, just tell me what to do and I'll do it."

"Can you get me work?" he asked through tears and sarcasm.

"No, but I can pick up extra shifts at the hospital to make some extra money. Do you think that will help?"

It didn't. Bob's depression deepened as his hours in front of the television grew.

When the solution came to me, it was so simple I wondered what had taken me so long to think of it in the first place. *A child,* I thought. *I will give him a child. After all, I reasoned, wasn't a child the only other thing he'd ever wanted?*

Once I decided to have a child, life moved very quickly. Ten days after I stopped taking birth-control pills, I was pregnant. Six weeks later the doctor confirmed what I already knew.

Bob was ecstatic with the news. "Annie, this is fantastic!"

I breathed a huge sigh of relief. "Then you're happy?"

"I'm beyond happy! I'm thrilled, amazed, overjoyed!"

And he was . . . for a while. But within weeks his depression returned and this time, when it came it brought along a new companion. Anger.

"Whatever possessed you to get pregnant?" he yelled as we drove home from the shopping mall with my first maternity dress.

"How could you have been so stupid? We can hardly afford ourselves. How are we ever going to afford a baby?"

The intensity of his outburst frightened me. "Please, don't yell at me. I'm so nauseated right now I can hardly stand it." I rolled down the car window and let the cool breeze blow over my face.

"You're not going to throw up, are you?"

I shook my head. The nausea had passed. "No, everything's going to be fine."

But everything wasn't fine.

In the third month of my pregnancy I hemorrhaged, and after that nothing was ever fine again.

The obstetrician stood at my bedside, his starched white lab coat covering his green scrub suit.

"You've lost a lot of blood, Anne, and I don't think we can wait much longer. I'd like to take you to surgery and do a simple D&C. Then we can send you home in the morning." His arms were crossed and he spoke so softly it was hard to hear what he was saying.

I knew that he was telling me I'd lost the baby, but I couldn't bring myself to believe it. Angry, frustrated, and overwhelmed with sadness, I started to cry. "But if you do the surgery, that'll be the end of everything."

"Well, yes, but it's the only way we have to stop the bleeding."

I looked away and stared at the intravenous fluid dripping rapidly through the tubing.

"Why is the IV going so fast?"

"Because, we have to try and make up for all the blood you lost."

"Oh, right. I guess I don't have my clinical brain on right now." I reached for the tissue from the bedside stand. I didn't care how much blood I'd lost. I wanted this baby, and if there was still a chance I could save the pregnancy, I wanted to take it. My head told me it was already too late, but my heart still held onto a whisper of hope.

"Can't we wait a little longer?"

"How much longer?"

"Maybe an hour or two?"

"An hour or two is a long time."

"I know that. But, we already know the bleeding has slowed down. Maybe if you just give me a little more time it'll stop completely."

"What makes you think it will stop?"

"I don't know." I blew my nose. "I just do."

Dr. Smith didn't answer. He seemed to be weighing every possible outcome. "Alright, Anne, but if things haven't sufficiently quieted down in a couple of hours you're going to surgery."

Bob looked sad and uncomfortable as Dr. Smith walked out of the room. "Do you want to watch some television?"

I nodded my head but soon discovered I'd lost my ability to concentrate. I watched the clock and monitored my body. The seconds turned into minutes. The nurses came in and checked me. The minutes turned into hours.

"It stopped," I whispered to Bob.

"Are you sure?"

"I'm sure."

"How do you know?"

"I just know. That's all. I just know." I said a silent prayer of simple gratitude. "Thank you, God. Thank you."

Dr. Smith walked back into my room exactly two hours later. "The nurses tell me you've stopped bleeding."

I nodded my head and tried in vain to smile.

"That's good. But I'd still like you to spend tonight and tomorrow night in the hospital. Let's just see how you do. I don't want you to become overly optimistic. The amount of blood you've lost has traumatized you as well as the baby. The baby may already be dead. "

My heart lurched in response to the doctor's casual soft bluntness. "How will I know if the baby's alive or not?"

"If it's alive, the baby will grow. It's that simple, Anne. Time will tell." And with that Dr. Smith turned and left.

Bob leaned over and stroked my hair. "I wish he were more reassuring."

"I do too, but he's supposed to be the best. All the nurses in the ICU go to him and I think that's always a good sign. Why don't you go home and get some rest now?"

"Are you sure?"

"I'm sure. And when you get home, would you check our insurance policy? I don't think I've worked here long enough to qualify for coverage."

"Annie, I'll do whatever I have to do to get you through this."

But I was right. We weren't covered. Twenty-four hours later I was back home. One week later I was back at work and everything went right back to the way it was before I was hospitalized with one exception. Now, every twinge sent shock waves through my body. Every cramp spelled potential disaster. If I'd hemorrhaged once, it could happen again.

Quitting my job was not an option. Bob needed to find work and work was not forthcoming.

In desperation I sat in the nurse's lounge one evening and drew up a list of all the people who I thought might help him.

Some were in the entertainment industry in Los Angeles, some still lived in Minneapolis. Some would never be able to give him work, but all could give him emotional support. Secretly I wrote and called them all.

Ted Mann, the owner of several movie theaters in Minneapolis before moving west and becoming a successful movie producer, was the first to respond.

I agreed to meet him at his production office at Warner Brothers. He was charming, gracious, and very sympathetic to our situation. But his words were hard to hear.

"Anne, I've known Bob since he was a young man and I certainly can't blame him for wanting to try it out here. He's got a lot of talent, but he waited too long. You've got to get him to go back. They don't need or want him out here. Nobody knows him and too many guys are already doing what he's trying to do. You'll be able to have a life in Minneapolis. Out here you'll have nothing."

The others I met all echoed Ted Mann's words.

"We like Bob. He's a talented guy. Get him to go back."

Calls started coming to the house, all from Minneapolis and all for Bob.

Bob didn't understand why all of these people were suddenly calling and it never occurred to him to ask me if I had anything to do with it. Finally, the call I'd been hoping for arrived. A Minneapolis agent phoned with an offer for work. They needed a director for a summer musical at the Theodore Roosevelt National Park. The park was located in Medora, a town we never heard of, and in North Dakota, a state we never wanted to visit.

"What should I do, Annie?" Bob asked after he'd hung up the phone.

I gave him two words of advice, "Take it."

Chapter Ten

Where Were You?

Two weeks after Bob accepted the job in North Dakota and one month before the baby was due, another hemorrhage launched me into premature labor. Three hours later I delivered an almost clinically dead baby girl and the delivery room erupted into organized chaos.

"Get the crash cart and get her pediatrician over here right now!" Dr. Smith sounded angry. What had gone wrong?

Through a medicated haze I stared at my new daughter. "Why is she so blue?" I asked. No one answered.

I pushed myself up onto my elbows. "I want to know why she's blue!"

I heard someone shout. "Get her back on that table!"

A nurse appeared at my side. "Anne, lie down."

I stayed upright. "No. I want to know what's wrong with her."

Then for just a split second the air in the room stood still. Everyone it seemed had heard the same sound.

It was more like a peep from a small bird than a human cry, but soon it was followed by a second heartier cry and with that the tension of the room melted away.

I eased my body back onto the delivery room table.

"Can I hold her now?"

"Anne." It was the nurse who'd told me to lie down. "Your baby needs a little extra attention. You'll be able to see her after we take you to your room."

"But she's going to be okay, isn't she?"

"She's going to be just fine," the doctor cut in. "Who knows where her husband is?"

The nurse handed Dr. Smith an instrument. "We've been calling their house for the last three hours. No one answers."

No one had been able to find Bob. Multiple phone calls to the house had yielded nothing. I didn't know where he was either, but I knew where he'd be at the end of my shift: waiting for me in the lobby of the hospital. He always was. In anticipation of his arrival, I gave a description of him to one of the staff nurses.

"Where have you been?" I cried when at last he rushed through the recovery room doors. "We had a baby girl and you missed everything!"

Bob leaned over the side rails of the gurney, his body convulsed in sobs. "You're not going to believe this, Annie, but I was so depressed I went for a long run tonight hoping I could give myself a heart attack. I'm sorry I missed everything, but how was I to know this would happen? The baby wasn't due for another month."

Once again the feeling of rage, my old childhood companion, resurrected itself. Soon the worlds inside my body started to collide and I gave in the difficult labor, delivery, and pain medication.

I no longer wanted to be strong and I didn't care what Bob had to say. I couldn't even muster the strength to care that he was there. "You know something, Bob? I'm really tired. Could you make the phone calls to everybody when you get home?" My words sounded mumbled. My mind, I knew, was slipping off the horizon.

"Sure, Annie, whatever you say. I love you so much."

I saw his mouth moving but his voice sounded very far away. I turned my head away and closed my eyes.

An hour later, still groggy from the medication, the nurses transferred me to my room. "Can you wheel me by the nursery first?" I asked as they pushed the gurney down the hall.

"Of course, we can. But remember, Dr. Smith told you your baby needs to be in the ICU for a couple of days."

"I just want to see my baby."

Through the large plate glass window in front of the ICU I stared at my new daughter as she lay motionless in an oversized isolette. "Why is she breathing so fast?"

"She has respiratory problems. Remember?"

"But she's going to be fine, right?"

"She's going to be fine. Your pediatrician's on his way over here right now."

"Oh, that's good. What time is it, anyway?"

"It's one in the morning."

"Really?" My words still sounded slightly slurred. "I'm in such a fog I can't keep anything straight. Dr. Baker is coming here? Now?"

"Yes. He should be here any minute."

"That's nice." I lowered myself onto the gurney. "We're going to call her Kimberly Anne . . . Kim for short." I wanted to say her name. I wanted someone to know my terribly sick baby had a name. *Maybe,* I thought, *maybe if I say her name she'll be able to hear the sound of my voice and gather strength.*

As it turned out Kim astonished everyone with her rapid improvement. She was transferred from the ICU into the main nursery two days after she was born and the following day was healthy enough to be discharged. She was released to us on the condition we bring her back to the hospital to have blood work and checkups. That was fine with me. I just wanted to get her home.

Six weeks later she was given a clean bill of health.

Bob was scheduled to start rehearsals in North Dakota the third week of June and that meant we had three hard days of driving in a car without air-conditioning if we were going to make it in time. But, Kim's arrival had literally charmed his sadness away.

"See," I told him as we headed east out of Los Angeles. "I was right. Having the baby was really good for you."

CHAPTER ELEVEN

God is Punishing Us

The summer passed quickly. Bob enjoyed the work, the show was a success and Kim remained healthy. But, I was tired all the time. No matter how many hours I slept, fatigue dogged my every waking hour. I blamed it on childbirth. "I guess having a baby's a lot tougher than I thought it would be," I told Bob one afternoon late in July.

I was right about the baby, but wrong about the reason for being tired. Unaware that the marriage had already begun to drain me, I had no way of knowing that it would be years before I'd ever feel rested again.

Still our spirits were high as we headed back to Los Angeles in September. *Maybe,* we thought, *just maybe things would be different this time.* And actually this time they were.

Bob was hired to direct two community choirs and even managed to find occasional work as a singer.

There was no hint of a depression threatening to make its way back into our lives and even though I was back at work full-time, life had begun to ease up.

And then Kim got sick. She was diagnosed with pneumonia. She weathered that crisis only to be struck down ten days later with another.

Soon she was caught in a vicious cycle: one week of good health would be followed by a two-week bout of pneumonia. Multiple medications helped, but there was little the pediatricians could do to keep her from getting sick. Each new illness intensified the dark circles under her eyes and each week they grew darker.

Bob's anger and frustration increased when each visit to the doctor's office failed to produce a cure. "What's wrong with those guys, anyway?" he yelled one afternoon when Kim came down with yet another cold.

"The doctors are doing all they can," I told him. Though in truth, I'd begun to wonder if they really were.

Finally one morning at the breakfast table he announced, "I know why this is happening to Kim."

"You do," I asked exhausted from another all night vigil at Kim's bedside.

"Yes, I do. God is punishing us for having dated while I was married."

I couldn't believe what he was saying. I watched as my breakfast cereal turned soggy. Did God really punish small children for the sins of the parents? And what about forgiveness?

Bob and I attended the Baptist church every Sunday and every Sunday we asked God to forgive us for our sins. Didn't the Bible say we worshipped a merciful God?

Throughout our entire relationship, in spite of all my doubts, I'd always believed that Bob was a better Christian than I was.

It was Bob who knew the Bible, not me. It was Bob who knew the specific time and date he'd been saved, not me.

And as if I needed further proof, Bob was the one who could stand up in front of a group of people to proclaim the gospel and challenge them to accept Jesus Christ as their Savior, not me. Who was I to challenge him on anything? I had a very simple belief system. Did Jesus love me? Yes. Had He died for my sins? Yes. Had He forgiven me for my sins? I'd certainly hoped so. But that was about it. Hardly the kind of faith I needed to do intellectual battle with anybody, much less a formidable opponent like Bob. But in spite of all that, I felt a stirring in my heart. Like a mother lioness sensing danger I was determined to protect Kim. She was not going to be the life-long bearer of what I thought was Bob's guilt—not God's punishment. "You can't possibly believe that, Bob. Kimmy's just a little girl. God wouldn't do that."

"Oh yes, He would. And if you read the Bible a little more often you'd find out what I'm talking about. If Kim's going to get well, we need to ask God's forgiveness for our adulterous affair."

Unable to deal with my fatigue and his sarcasm any longer, I exploded.

"We've already asked for His forgiveness a thousand times! How many times do we have to do this?"

"We'll have to do it until he takes this curse off our lives. I think that's probably the reason I'm not getting work. Just look at all the people God's blessing. He's blessing everyone but me. Even Dean Martin has his own show."

"What has Dean Martin got to do with anything? Besides, I think God is blessing us. Look at Kim. You wanted a child all your life and now you have one."

"Yes. But she's sick and it's our fault."

"I think that's something you're choosing to believe. You thought you'd have a career as big as Dean Martin's and because you don't, you have to blame somebody. I don't know why Kimmy's sick, but I think the doctors are going to find the answer."

"Right."

"What is wrong with you, anyway?"

"She's not getting any better. Is she?"

It was true, she wasn't. But I still didn't think Bob was right.

"Is she?"

"Since you seem to be the one with all the answers, what do you think I should do?"

He got up from the kitchen table and picked up Kim from her highchair. "You need to pray more. You need to pray more and ask God to forgive you."

"Fine. I'll pray more and ask God to forgive me . . . again."

• • •

Two long years later Kim was referred to a Pediatric Allergist and after a lengthy diagnostic process, was found to be allergic to the California tree pollens growing outside her bedroom window. The allergy shots she received were frequent and painful, but once she was in treatment, her health steadily improved.

Eventually, the years of our life fell into a pattern. September through May we lived in Los Angeles, June through August were spent in North Dakota.

I lived for the summers. In Medora, I had a husband who loved his work and a daughter who was healthy.

But every Labor Day Los Angeles sang her siren song, and like lemmings rushing to their death in the sea, we returned to search out our destiny. I still thought, as did Bob, that it would only be a matter of time until success was his.

And then disaster struck.

It was late in September and we'd returned from North Dakota the week before, hopeful there would be work waiting for him when we arrived. There was good news. People were now returning his phone calls. And there was bad. There was still no work.

On the evening disaster struck I'd left all the doors to the house open, hoping to catch last rays of fall sunlight for the day when suddenly the landscape of my mind changed forever. A random thought, *what if nothing ever changes,* exploded in my brain as I stood at the stove stirring spaghetti sauce. That was followed in quick succession by, *what if he never finds a job?* And then like colliding bumper cars at the county fair, my thoughts started smashing into one another. *What if we have to live on my nurse's salary for the rest of my life,* crashed into, *maybe we waited too long.* And finally the most frightening of all, *what if he actually fails?*

Beads of sweat popped out on my upper lip. I had to get myself under control. I had to calm down. If I didn't, these thoughts that had leaped full-blown into my head would take on a life of their own.

Total and complete faith in Bob was the glue that held our relationship together. Anything less was betrayal. I'd worshipped at the altar of Bob's talent for so long that these thoughts were tantamount to heresy.

Calm down, Anne. You've got to calm down. Everything's going to be fine. You know he's going to succeed. He has too much talent to fail. Everybody says so.

The spaghetti sauce bubbled out onto the stove. "It's just

going to take longer than we thought, that's all," I murmured as I turned down the gas flame to a simmer.

"Why are you looking at me like that?" Bob asked once we were seated at the dinner table.

I forced myself to sound casual. "Like what?"

"I don't know like what. It feels like you're studying me or something."

"I was just thinking how much better it's been for you since you've picked up so many performing jobs with your choirs." I couldn't stop fiddling and twisting my hair.

"Yeah, but it's not why I came out here."

I gave him my most reassuring smile but I had sprung a leak, and I knew it.

CHAPTER TWELVE

Get a Job . . . Any Job

In spite of everything, or maybe because of everything, we decided to have another child. I loved being a mother and even though Bob was proving to be a marginal parent at best, it was obvious to everyone that he adored Kim. With twinkling brown eyes and curly brown hair just like her father's, Kim was bright, funny and inquisitive. She was a joy to watch and a delight to be around.

When the second pregnancy was confirmed, I had high hopes that it would be different from the first. And it was, though not in the ways in which I had expected.

The fatigue, which had begun years earlier in North Dakota, now became unending. I woke up tired and went to bed exhausted. The nausea and vomiting, so common in the initial stages of pregnancy, stayed through the fifth month and eventually my despair surpassed anything I'd ever known.

Six months into the pregnancy I awoke early one morning and stared at the sleeping form of my husband. The longer I stared the more annoyed I became.

How could he sleep when every day we sank deeper and deeper into debt? Why wasn't he exhausted? Why wasn't he the one full-time instead of me?

I shook him awake. "Bob."

"Annie, what is it?" His voice was groggy with sleep.

"I need you to get a job. I don't care what kind of job it is so long as it brings in money."

His eyes flew open. "You want to run that by me again?"

I got out of bed and reached for my robe. "I said . . . I need you to get a job."

"And just what kind of job did you have in mind?"

"You can be a security guard for all I care. Do whatever it takes to start bringing in some steady money."

He bolted upright. "So," he spat out as he sat on the edge of the bed. "You've lost faith in me."

"No," I lied. "I just need some help. That's all. I'm really tired."

"Well, you wouldn't be so tired if you hadn't gotten pregnant again."

I glared at him. "This pregnancy was a joint decision, remember? Now will you just get some kind of job, so I don't have to work so hard?"

"I'm going to make it as an artist," he exploded. "I will not jeopardize my chances for success by getting a nine-to-five job! You know as well as I do that I need to leave that time open for auditions."

I heard Kim's feet running down the hallway towards the living room and the sounds of *Sesame Street* soon came drifting through the bedroom door. I tied my robe over my swollen body. "I need you to get a job. Okay?"

Our quarrels had begun.

One bright spot did soon appear. Bob had somehow managed to book a singing and speaking tour for the Knife and Fork Club Agency out of Kansas.

They'd hired him to entertain the Kiwanis and Rotary Clubs across America and even though it meant he'd be leaving ten days before my due date, we knew he had to take it. We'd run out of options and we were running out of money.

Our second daughter was born one week after Bob left, and this time I didn't need anyone to tell me something was wrong. I could tell just by looking at her.

The pediatrician's exam confirmed what I'd already suspected. "Anne, your baby needs to be evaluated by the specialists at Children's Hospital."

Fear made it difficult for me to speak. I couldn't get my mouth to form the words. My tongue felt thick. "What do you think is wrong with her?" I asked with great effort.

"I'm not sure. It may be nothing more than a really rough delivery."

"And, if it isn't?"

"Then she may need some surgery, but we're getting ahead of ourselves. Why don't we wait to see what the doctors at Children's have to say?"

"When do you want me to do this?"

"Just as soon as you're discharged. Do you think you can do that?"

Unable to speak, I simply nodded my head yes. The phone rang as the doctor was leaving the room.

I cleared my throat before answering. "Hello?"

"Annie?" It was Bob and he was sobbing. "When you didn't answer the phone I started calling everyone. Mother just told me we had a baby girl."

My hostility went undisguised. "I told you not to start calling everyone. Remember? I said if you couldn't find me at home, I'd be at the hospital. We don't have the money for you to be making all these long distance phone calls. And stop crying, will you? You always cry when you feel bad for yourself. You have spent more time crying than any man I know."

"I should have been there, Annie. I should have been there."

"I know that. But one of us has to work and as surprising as this may seem to you, it's your turn. I've named her Christina, Tina, actually. I like that name and unless you have some big objection to it, that's what it's going to be."

"Christina is fine. It's perfect."

"Bob, please don't call me again unless you can stop crying."

The phone wires pulsated with tension.

"Annie, is everything alright?"

"Yes."

"I'll call you tomorrow."

"No, don't. We'll be checking out."

"You know I love you, don't you?"

"Yes."

"Well, I guess I'll let you get your rest. I'll be praying for you, Annie."

"Fine." My voice cracked. "You do that." I hung up the phone and pushed the nurses call light.

Within seconds a voice came over the speaker above my head.

"Can I help you?"

There was so much pain in my heart I thought if I started to cry I'd be crying for years. "Could someone bring my baby into my room? I know I told you I wanted her to stay in the main nursery, but I've changed my mind."

There was a long pause before I heard, "Someone will be right down."

The nurse wheeled the bassinet into my room. "Do you feel comfortable feeding her by yourself or would you like me to stay with you?"

"I'm fine," I answered, my chin quivering. "I'm really fine."

As I watched the nurse walk away I wanted to scream, "Stop! Don't go! Please don't leave me here alone! " But I let her walk out of the room in silence.

Inching my way out of bed, I walked over to the bassinet and stared at the small bundle wrapped in a pink blanket. *She looks so normal,* I thought. Then suddenly, the baby let out a plaintive cry. I stared at her. Her cry grew louder.

I heard a voice inside my head say, "pick her up." But I did nothing. The second time the voice spoke, it was louder. "Pick her up!" And still I didn't move. The third time it sounded a command. "I said pick her up!"

With halting moves I reached into the bassinet and picked up my newborn daughter. I caressed Tina's deformed head. I kissed her eye, which had been pushed so far back into the socket it almost looked as if her eye was missing.

I gently patted her tiny bottom with the dislocated hip and placed my now tear-stained cheek next to her fractured collarbone and twisted neck muscle. "God's got to get us through this, Tina. There isn't anybody else who can."

Then I looked into my daughter's face and softly asked, "Are you hungry? Is that why you're crying? Are you hungry?"

I awoke with a start at six the next morning. The phone was ringing.

"Yes?"

"Mommy is that you? It doesn't sound like you."

I breathed a huge sigh of relief. It wasn't Bob. "Kimmy, you're calling so early. Is everything okay?"

"No. It's not. When are you coming to get me? I don't like it here."

"I'll be there just as soon as I can. How did you know how to call me?"

"Thea dialed the phone for me."

"Thea? Wanda's daughter?"

"Uh huh." Kim started to cry. "I don't want to stay here anymore. You've got to come and get me right now."

"Are they being mean to you?"

"No."

"Are you hungry?"

"No. Wanda says we'll have breakfast after I talk to you."

"Kimmy, honey, please don't cry. I'll be there just as soon as I can. Did you know you have a new baby sister?"

I could hear Kim's small sobs but she said nothing.

"Kim?"

"What?"

"Did Wanda tell you that you have a new baby sister?"

"I'm nodding my head. Can't you hear me?"

"No, honey I can't. Kimmy, could you put the phone down for a second and go get Wanda? I need to talk to her for a second. I promise I'll be there just as soon as I can."

"Okay." The receiver clattered to the floor.

My friend Wanda and I had worked together on the same surgical unit for the past three years and when it became apparent that Bob was going to be out of town for the delivery, Wanda quickly volunteered to take care of Kim.

"Hi, Anne," Wanda said as she picked up the receiver off the floor.

The sound of her cheerful voice calmed my anxious heart.

"Wanda, could you do me a huge favor? I need to take Tina to Children's Hospital this morning. I know that it's Sunday and everything, but they want her examined before they send her home with me. I called Bob's family, but none of them can do it because they have church today. And . . . "

"Anne, whatever you need, I can do. When do you want to go?"

"I have an appointment at eleven. I don't think it'll take very long, but I'm not sure."

"Don't worry about how long it takes. What time do you want me there?"

"Ten?"

"I'll be there. Kim's not going to like this very much. She's terribly homesick, but she'll do fine with my two older girls here."

"Should I talk to her again?"

"No, you don't have to do that. Our dog Muffin had a litter last week and she's been fascinated with the new puppies. You have enough to worry about."

Children's Hospital of Los Angeles was only a short car ride away and once the nurse had taken Tina into the Radiology Department, there was nothing left for us to do but wait. Wanda and I sat side by side in the reception room until a tall angular man wearing a long white lab coat walked in. "Who is Christina's mother?"

I stood up. "I am."

He extended his hand. "I'm Dr. MacNamara, one of the radiologists here. Please sit down. I've been going over your daughter's x-rays." He sat down in the chair across from me. "I've also reviewed them with a neurosurgeon and orthopedist, and I think I have some very good news for you. There are some things here that need to be corrected, but what we have here is the best possible outcome we could've hoped for."

The tears started coming faster that I could keep up with them. Wanda began passing me tissues until she finally handed me the entire box.

"I know this isn't easy," Dr. MacNamara said with genuine concern. "So let me start by telling you what she doesn't need.

"She doesn't need to have surgical intervention for anything. Time should take care of easing her head and face into proper proportion. Things are terribly misaligned, but everything is there. Her fractured collarbone won't be a problem. It will heal very quickly on its own. She does, however, need to be under orthopedic care for her dislocated hip and shortened neck muscles. You can take her home today as long as you make arrangements to have her seen by the end of the week. Now I understand you're a nurse, so you are probably familiar with most of these things. Do you have any questions I can answer for you?"

"Yes. Do you know why this happened? Was it something I did?"

"I don't know your history at all, so I'm probably not the best qualified person to answer this, but it looks to me like most of this is due to a really rough delivery."

"Even the hip?"

"No." He shook his head. "Nobody knows why those things happen. Fortunately, her hip displacement isn't very severe and doesn't look like it's going to require surgery. So you're lucky in that regard. Do you have someone in mind for orthopedic care?"

"Yes."

"Well, I guess that's it then. In just a moment one of the

nurses will bring your daughter out and if I can be of any further help in the future, let me know."

It wasn't long before Wanda had us back at the house and settled in. Along the way she'd stopped at the grocery store and purchased food for the week.

"At least I know you guys won't be starving," she said as she unloaded the bags of groceries. "Now you're sure you want me to bring Kim home after dinner? As much as I love that kid of yours, both you and I know she can be quite a handful."

I smiled for the first time that day. "Yeah, I know. She keeps me busy. But she's so homesick I think it would be better for everybody."

"Alright, then I'll see you tonight."

Later that evening Kim and I stood in the doorway and waved goodbye to Wanda. "Do we have to keep her?"

"Keep who, honey?"

She pointed in the direction of the bedroom. "That baby."

"Of course we have to keep her. She's part of our family now."

"Well, I don't want her. Send her back."

"We can't send her back. I wouldn't even if I could. Do you want to see her?" I closed the door and took Kim's hand.

"No."

"Tina brought you a present." I smiled in hopes of winning her over. "Don't you want to see what it is?"

Her four year old face wore a look of disgust. "Don't be stupid. Everybody knows babies don't have the money to buy presents."

"Well, the present is on the sofa in case you change your mind. Why don't you see what's on television. And Kim?"

She turned and scowled. "What?"

"Tina's not going anywhere."

She burst into tears. "I miss my Daddy! I wish he were here. I'd rather have him than that stupid baby."

"Daddy's not coming home for a very long time. He's working, remember? But we can call him tomorrow. Would you like to do that?"

Her face lit up. "Can we call him now?"

"No, sweetheart, he's working now. We'll do it in the morning."

She turned and walked towards the television set dragging her favorite threadbare blanket behind her.

That night as I slid my exhausted body between the cool sheets of my bed, tears from my closed eyelids formed a steady stream down onto my pillow.

It had all been too much: Tina's birth, the trip to Children's Hospital, Bob's phone call. I wanted to be strong, but my strength was gone. Fatigue, both emotional and physical, had drained it away. I needed sleep but my mind was on a rampage.

Tina had such a soft little cry. What if she woke up and I didn't hear her? What time was it, anyway? I sat up and grabbed the clock off the dresser. The illuminated green numbers said it was nine o'clock. I couldn't remember when I'd last fed Tina. How much time did I have before she'd need to eat again? Was it hours? If I had two hours then I could take a nap. That's it. I'll just nap for a couple of hours. You're going to be fine, Anne. The girls are going to be fine. God's going to get you through this. You know He will. And always in the back of my mind a terrible thought stalked my every waking hour.

What if He didn't?

"Here," the obstetrician said as he handed me a prescription for Valium. "This should do the trick." But it didn't. I was twenty-eight years old and so tired I thought I was dying. I called on Wanda more and more. She started to worry.

"Things will get back to normal soon," I told her. But I knew that normal had ceased to exist for me a long time ago.

"Fine," I told Bob every time he called home. "Everyone's just fine." Why tell him anything else? He was never any help and I no longer had the energy to deal with him. It took all the energy I had just to get Tina to her doctor appointments and deal with Kim's unrelenting hostility.

In one respect time was working in our favor. Tina's appearance was improving daily. Bumps and bruises from the delivery slowly disappeared and eventually, her neck muscles returned to their normal position. Within weeks she was able to turn her head in both directions and no longer whimpered when you picked her up. When we met Bob at the airport five weeks later, Tina still wore a hip brace, but in every other way resembled a normal looking baby. God had come through for us.

"It's my family," Bob shouted when he saw us waiting in the terminal. "Let me see her! I want to see my new daughter."

I placed Tina in his arms.

His look of surprise and confusion was instantaneous. "What's wrong with her?"

"She's wearing a hip brace, Daddy," Kim announced with great authority. "She has to wear it so she won't have a limp when she starts to walk."

Bob's eyes turned frantic. "But she's going to be alright? Isn't she, Annie?"

"She's going to be fine. Let's go get your luggage."

"Sure, Annie, anything you say."

As we made our way to the baggage claim area Bob stopped anyone who'd listen. "This is my new daughter," he'd exclaim. "She's five weeks old and it's the first time I've seen her." No one turned away. Everyone responded with smiles and kind words. I hated every minute of it.

I hated Bob's showmanship in ordinary circumstances. I hated how much attention he needed from total strangers. One person waiting at the luggage carousel constituted an audience and he'd do whatever it took to garner his or her affection. I didn't want our family to be part of his act. We were not a happy family, although that is exactly what he wanted these strangers to believe. I didn't acknowledge their smiles. I couldn't. My jaw was aching from my clenched teeth.

I waited until the children were in bed for the night before I turned to Bob and said, "We need to talk."

Bob sat across from me on the sofa. "Annie, don't sound serious. I have something I want to give you. Come sit next to me." He patted the sofa.

"This chair is fine."

He shrugged his shoulders and got up to hand me a small gift- wrapped package. "This doesn't come close to telling you how much I love you, but I hope you like it just the same."

I opened the box. Inside was a small silver cross with a miniature diamond chip in the center. I couldn't bring myself to look at him. "You left the price tag on it. It says it cost sixteen-dollars and ninety-five cents."

"But it's what you wanted, right?"

I found it impossible to lift my head. "Yes," I said as I stared at the price tag. "This is what I asked for, but I can't believe you paid so little for it. It looks like something you'd give to a young girl."

"I thought you'd be pleased." His voice cracked. "I'm surprised you're so disappointed."

My head snapped up. "Are you going to start crying again?"

"No! Annie, I don't understand why you're so angry."

"I'm angry because I always have to handle everything by myself! I'm angry because I gave birth to our second daughter without you. But most of all I'm angry with myself. I can't believe that even after all these years I was still hoping you'd come home with something wonderful. Is this all I'm worth to you? Sixteen dollars and ninety-five cents?"

"I think you've said enough! You were the one that told me to take this job. If you didn't want me to be out on the road you should've told me to stay home long before I left. You know, Annie, somehow I thought my bringing in some money was going to make you happy. After all, you're the one who's always complaining about how broke we are. And as for the necklace . . . I bought you exactly what you asked for. If you don't like it, give it to one of the girls."

I got up from the chair and walked out of the room in silence.

The walls were closing in from every side.

CHAPTER THIRTEEN

Two for the Price of One

My prayer life rapidly deteriorated into one-line directives and begging. "Help me," turned into "Please God, you've got to help me." And finally, "Please, please, please God. You've got to help me." I thought if I begged God long enough, and hard enough, He'd come to my rescue. Clearly, somebody had to rescue me. I was drowning in a roiling sea of my own anger and so consumed with rage I couldn't stand to be in my own skin. And then overnight my ability to concentrate simply vanished.

"Think, Anne, think," I muttered to myself several times a day in hopes of retrieving a vital piece of information that had somehow slipped off the mental Rolodex of my brain. It helped to talk to myself. But not much. I switched jobs thinking it would relieve the unending pressure building in my chest. It didn't.

Finally, in a move that may have appeared miniscule to those outside the fundamental belief system but was huge to me, I searched for and found a women's Bible study . . . at a Presbyterian Church.

I chose Bel-Air Presbyterian Church because of a long held desire to attend ever since Bob had been a guest choral conductor one Sunday morning on our honeymoon, but I knew there was little chance I'd be able to go the church on a regular basis.

Bob would never have allowed it. Even though our daily devotional time had ended long ago, he still enforced the strict rules of the fundamental Baptist belief system, and in this case that meant he chose the church we attended. A Presbyterian Church, unless he had been hired as their Minister of Music, would've been out of the question.

But I was tired of learning about the teachings of the church as told to me by Bob. I was sick of hearing him say that God had forgotten about us or that we'd been cursed, and I didn't believe him anymore when he said God hadn't forgiven us. One disturbing question began to surface with greater and greater frequency. *Am I losing my faith in God?* My life was racing towards the precipice of disaster, and still it would take another two years before I was finally able to admit to myself what I'd suspected all along. I wasn't losing faith in God. I was only losing faith in Bob.

From the moment I walked into the sanctuary for my first Tuesday morning Bible Study my life started to change. And I still remember how it felt to this day. All I have to do is see the chapel in my mind and I am immediately transported back in time.

I still see the sunlight flowing through the high stained glass windows as it bathed the room in warm colors of amber and light blue . . . the friendly chatter of the women . . . the woodcarvings of Jesus over the altar . . .I can see it all.

When a small slender woman with streaks of gray running through her dark brown hair came over and introduced herself to me as Margaret, I was appreciative. It made me feel welcome. I told her she looked lovely. And she did.

Dressed in a light gray and white pantsuit with a pearl necklace and matching pearl button earrings, everything about her said confidence. I knew instantly whatever it was she had, I wanted. It was only after everyone had settled in that I realized who she was. Margaret was the Bible study teacher.

When I decided to return the following Tuesday, I already knew what Bob was going to say to me. He'd say that he was completely in favor of my going to a Bible study—as long as it was at the Baptist church we attended on Sunday mornings. He'd also find a scripture verse to remind me that since God had made him spiritual head of the household, I would be allowed to go to the Tuesday Morning Bible Study only on an occasional basis. Anything more and I would be challenging his God given authority over me.

But my war for independence had begun and my timing couldn't have been worse.

Two months after I'd made my initial strike for freedom, Bob temporarily put aside his quest for fame in the secular world and decided to go full time as a Minister of Music at Valley Baptist Church, the second largest Baptist church in the San Fernando Valley.

"This will be the last Bible study you'll be able to attend at that precious church of yours," he announced one Tuesday morning as the girls and I were heading out the door.

I stared at him but said nothing in response. It was pointless to try and tell him anything.

He'd always find a scripture verse to back up why he was

right and I was wrong. In recent months I'd fallen back on the old habit I'd perfected years earlier with my mother. I gave him "the look." It was the only defense I had and it still worked.

"Oh, you can look at me anyway you want, but you're still not going to be able to go there anymore. When I took this job, they didn't just hire me. They hired us. I told them at the interview that they'd get 'two for the price of one.' This has been my biggest chance for success since we moved here and you're not going to blow it for me. "

I ignored him and proceeded out the door.

His voice got louder. "What is wrong with you? Don't you know you're going against what the Bible teaches?"

The girls and I kept walking. "You know something? I'm only beginning to learn what the Bible teaches and so far I haven't run into anything that says we have to go to the same church."

"Annie, why are you doing this to me?" It was a lament that I would hear often over the years to come.

I stopped on the sidewalk. "It's very simple. This Bible study makes me happy and I'm starting to make friends."

"You can make friends at my church, and besides those people at your church are Presbyterians!"

"Now what's that supposed to mean?"

"You know what it means. It means they don't preach the true gospel."

"Well, here's what I think it means." My voice was getting tense and I let out an audible sigh in an attempt to reduce my rising anger. "I think it means this whole thing is all about you. I don't think this has anything to do with who preaches gospel and who doesn't." I continued. "You need me at your church because you need to look good. And for your information I don't care what you told them to get them to hire you. I'll still sing in one of your choirs but there's nothing you can do to stop me from going to Bel-Air on Tuesday mornings." The strength of my conviction began to flow from my voice to other parts of my body. I turned and walked the girls to the car.

I was no longer willing to do what Bob asked. Even if he did claim it was Scriptural, I no longer believed him. If God wanted me to follow specific rules and regulations as a wife, He was going to have to tell me Himself.

• • •

The stress in our marriage escalated.

A year passed.

A year filled with weekly Bible studies and marital turbulence, and when the turbulence became unbearable, I reached out to the only person I knew who held my admiration and respect. Margaret responded immediately, and overnight our relationship went from teacher and student, to confidant and friend.

Every week she prayed with me, and every week she listened to me cry. She encouraged me, supported me and told me to be strong, but most of all she said I wasn't alone.

In June of that same year I told Bob he was going to have to make our annual trip to North Dakota alone. It was a heart-wrenching decision.

Bob was afraid he'd never see the girls again. The girls were afraid they'd never "see Daddy again." And everybody was crying.

The never-ending phone calls started as soon as he stepped off the plane in North Dakota. Bob missed the girls.

Kim and Tina missed their father. Three weeks later I caved in.

But in spite of my efforts to bolster my confidence, I simply couldn't shake the sense of foreboding that had attached itself to my heart. *I hope I'm not making a huge mistake,* I thought to myself as the girls and I boarded the plane early one morning in Los Angeles and flew back to the Midwest.

Chapter Fourteen

She's Dead, Isn't She?

North Dakota can be either beautiful or barren depending on your perspective and where you happen to be standing at the moment. From where I stood in the summer of 1973, it was beautiful and the name notwithstanding, the rugged beauty of Medora and the Badlands bordered on breathtaking.

Each day begins with the sun in a brilliant bright blue sky radiating the days to perfection, and with the possible exception of an occasional passing thunderstorm, the calendar days of June and July pass by as flawless. All of that changes in mid-August, however, when daytime temperatures soar to one-hundred degrees and drop off to near freezing at night. It's nature's way of reminding us, lest the balmy days of summer charm everyone into forgetting that the endless cycle of the seasons still waits to play itself out.

On the day the first wild temperature swing occurred, I discovered the furnace in our sparsely furnished three-bedroom trailer wasn't working and set out on a short dusty walk into town to find Mr. Johnston, the town manager. He'd been helpful to us before and I was sure he would help us now.

The entire town of Medora was modeled after the Wild West, complete with hitching posts, horse drawn wagons, boarded sidewalks and a saloon. Almost everyone, including Mr. Johnston, wore Levi's, cowboy boots and plaid shirts.

I walked into his office with a confident smile on my face. I liked this man. "Do you think you can have someone fix our furnace?" I asked. "I don't want the children to be without heat at night."

"Seems sort of silly, don't you think? It's already August and you folks are going to be gone by Labor Day."

His response caught me off guard. "No. I don't. You know how cold the nights in August can get." I knew I sounded defensive but for reasons I couldn't explain, I suddenly felt afraid. I wanted that furnace fixed.

Mr. Johnston leaned his lanky frame against the back of the chair and rubbed his reddish-gray beard. "Okay, here's what I'm going to do. I'm going to give you a space heater and some extra blankets. That should take care of the problem. After you folks leave we're gonna be shuttin' everything down and may even sell off some of these mobile homes we have sittin' around here. No point in makin' extra work and wastin' money. Besides, the summer's been so hot this year I don't think you'll be missin' that furnace much at all."

When I told Bob about my conversation with Mr. Johnston, he was unconcerned.

"Well, let's just try it, Annie. We don't want to make too much work for them so close to the end of the summer."

Two hours later an outdated space heater arrived along with three extra blankets and for the next three weeks Mr. Johnston was right.

The summer remained unusually hot and we managed quite well without a furnace.

But in the early pre-dawn hours of the last week in August, winter made a premature arrival and forced five-and-a-half-year-old Kim from her bed to search for warmth. She didn't have to go far to find it. I'd placed the space heater with its red-hot coils glowing in the dark in the hallway next to her bedroom.

Smoke doesn't make any noise as it slithers under doorways and snakes its way through air vents. You have to be able to smell it before it kills you or someone you love. And on the night winter made its premature arrival, Bob and I smelled it. It jolted us out of bed and sent us running over the cold linoleum floor into the hallway. But even in our extreme heightened state of awareness and adrenalin pumping through our veins, we weren't prepared for the horror of what we saw. Kim was on fire. So was her pillowcase. So were the drapes. Her nightgown had brushed up against the space heater and it had ignited everything in its path. At first Bob attempted to put the fire out with his hands, but the flames only got worse.

I pushed him aside, grabbed Kim and leaped out the back door of the trailer. We hit the ground together and with one powerful pull I ripped off her flannel nightgown. One long agonizing scream tore through Kim's body, ricocheted off the mountains that surrounded us and disappeared into the silence of the cold night air.

Now the source of her pain was clearly visible. There wasn't any skin on her chest nor was there any on her right thigh.

The skin on her right arm was blackened up to the elbow. Her thumb was split open and there were smoke rings around her ear. And then her seared body began to shake.

At first it was nothing more than a tremor, but it gathered speed with terrifying intensity. Gripping her under her arm sockets, I hoisted her back into the smoke-filled trailer and hissed at Bob.

"Get Tina. Her room's filling up with smoke."

He did as he was told and after he placed Tina on the yellow vinyl kitchen-chair next to the phone, he stood in front of me and rapidly began shaking his hands.

"Bring the car around while I call the hospital," I barked. "And why are you shaking your hands like that?"

"I guess I burned them trying to put out the fire."

"Well, somehow, you're going to have to manage to drive the car," I snapped.

I was unmoved by Bob's pain. The flames that had set my daughter on fire had ignited a lifetime of anger, pain and resentment. In one terrifying moment everything had changed and my rage, like a giant tsunami, began taking out everything in its path. There simply wasn't any room left in the graveyard of my heart for compassion. All that space had been given away years ago.

Months later, it occurred to me that Bob probably didn't deserve the full impact of a lifetime of rage, but once I saw the flames shooting off of Kim's body I was powerless to contain it.

It would take years of therapy before I would come to understand that the fire that had nearly cost Kim her life had claimed each one of us. The flames that had nearly killed Kim had left us all with scorched hearts.

The car flew over Interstate 80 to the nearest hospital forty miles away and Kim, wrapped only in a sheet, sat between us and didn't move.

She was so still her breathing was barely audible. Eighteen-month-old Tina, dressed in her pink flannel snuggle-sack pajamas, sat huddled down in the corner of the backseat.

Bob's blistered hands had quickly filled with fluid, but he hardly noticed them. It was Kim's stillness that terrified him.

"Is she dead?" his voice trembled.

Unabated, my anger raged on. "No. She's not dead."

A mile passed. "Why don't you tell me the truth?" he pleaded. "She's dead, isn't she?"

Again I answered, "No. She's not dead."

But he wasn't convinced, and with each passing mile he'd ask again. And again. And again. Nothing I said reassured him. Finally, I whispered to Kim, "Honey, tell Daddy you're not dead."

"Daddy," Kim said in a voice so faint you had to strain to hear it, "I'm not dead."

Thirty minutes later we pulled into the hospital parking lot. It felt like it had taken a lifetime.

One week later I told the attending physician, "I've decided to take her back to Los Angeles."

"I want Kim to see the burn specialist at my hospital and I can give my daughter all the nursing care she's going to need." It was a risky decision. Kim still required daily baths and dressing changes, but my anger had just taken a quantum leap.

I now hated everything that I associated with the fire. Bob. The hospital. The doctor. I even hated the town. The only thing I wanted to do was get back to Los Angeles and never see North Dakota again. The doctor agreed to my request.

• • •

"Mommy, turn off the water!" Kim screamed through her tears.

We'd come to the most difficult part of day, the daily bath. Infection in any patient can be serious, but in a burn victim it can be fatal. Every new motel meant another daily bath and Kim hated every single one.

I sat down on the bed next to her. "Kimmy, honey, you know we've got to do this so you don't get infected."

"No! It hurts too much."

"But, you're doing so well! Your chest has almost healed. Your arm doesn't even need dressings on it anymore. It's just your leg now."

"No!" She jumped off the bed and limped over to Bob.

"Does she really have to do this?" Bob asked huddling the girls closer to him.

"Yes, she does! If she gets infected we're going to have another catastrophe on our hands. Now, will you please help me?"

"I can't, Annie. You're the nurse in the family not me."

"Then get out," I exploded. "And take Tina with you so she doesn't have to hear Kim screaming."

Bob picked up Tina and left the room.

We were alone now, Kim and I, and both of us were equally determined.

I walked over to the bed and just as I was about to pick her up, she summoned an enormous burst of energy and kicked me in the stomach. "I won't get in the tub and you can't make me!"

For several seconds both of us were so stunned that neither one of us moved. And then, with super-human resolve, and a brief prayer, I forcibly picked up my kicking and screaming daughter and carried her into the tub.

Three days later we sat in the office of Dr. A. Richard Grossman in Los Angeles.

"Congratulations," he said with a small nod in my direction. "She looks terrific. It's hard to believe that her burns were as extensive as her chart indicates. I think we should keep on doing the daily baths, but I can assure you that the worst is over."

But he was wrong. The worst wasn't over. That night a high piercing scream jolted us awake and sent me flying into Kim's room. But I was too late. She was already up and running through the house.

All of my initial attempts to catch her failed. Finally I lunged for her and held on tight just as she was reaching for the handle on the front door.

"Kimmy, can you hear me?" The strength in her body was enormous. "Kim, honey, you're not on fire anymore. You're home. You're safe."

Slowly, her thrashing subsided. I pressed on. "Kim, listen to Mommy. You're having a bad dream. You're home. You're safe. The fire is over. You just had a bad dream." Over and over I repeated, "You're home. You're safe. You're not on fire," until finally her breathing returned to normal and I carried her back to bed.

Tina peered out through the bars of her crib and watched me pull the covers back over Kim's sleeping body. "She's just had a bad dream," I said as I tenderly kissed each of the girls and walked back into my bedroom.

Bob sat on the edge of the bed searching my face for reassurance. "How is she?"

I climbed into bed and turned away from him. "She'll be fine."

And still it wasn't over. Kim was getting better but I was

getting worse. My rage had begun to abscess inside of me and soon I was emotionally unrecognizable, even to myself. Everything in daily life bothered me. I jumped at the slightest noise.

A truck passing me on the freeway brought tears to my eyes. The pressure and pain in my chest was almost unbearable. Everyday it felt like I was submitting to open-heart surgery without anesthesia. My headaches became non-stop. As soon as one would leave, another one would start. Sleep was impossible. Every night it was the same. Go to bed. Fall asleep. Wake up two hours later. Stay awake until dawn. Fall asleep. Get up with the girls at seven. And I cried all the time.

One month later, on the morning of what turned out to be Kim's third and final nightmare, I made a decision. I wanted out. Out of my marriage. Out of these claustrophobic feelings. Out from under this black cloud of oppression. Out. The fact that I had absolutely no idea how I was going to do this didn't change the fact I still wanted out.

CHAPTER FIFTEEN

Do You Really Think Someone Can Help Me?

When I told my Bible study group of my decision, I was so frightened I couldn't even say the word divorce. I told them I wanted a separation instead. Even so, just saying the word separation was so powerful that it was greeted by a wall of silence.

Unable to bear the heaviness in the air, I leaped to my own defense. "I know you think this is sudden. But, it's not. It's been on my mind for a long time." Silence.

Margaret, whose kind voice had soothed my jangled nerves many times over in the past year, came to my aide. "What Anne says is true. She has struggled in her marriage for a very long time." And then she turned to me. "Do you have some time after Bible study today, Anne? Perhaps we can talk."

I nodded my head yes. I didn't trust myself to speak.

"Nobody said anything," I wailed in Margaret's office as soon as the meeting was over. "I didn't even tell them what I really wanted."

"I know, dear. Your news frightened them. I'm actually a little surprised you didn't tell me first."

I ignored her mild reprimand. "Well, are they going to be like that forever?"

"Just give them time. They'll be calling you soon to show their support."

"I sure hope you're right."

"Anne, I've been thinking about how much you've been through lately and if you agree to it, I'd like you to see a friend of mine. He happens to be a psychologist."

"A psychologist? You want me to see a shrink? Why can't I just go on talking to you?"

"Because you and your whole family have been in a terrible crisis since the fire and I think you need someone with more expertise than I have."

I stared out the window. "Do you really think someone can help me?"

Margaret placed her arm around me and nodded her head. "Yes, dear, I do."

And with that, the unbearable weight of the world upon my shoulders began to lift.

Still, it took me three weeks to pick up the phone and call the therapist, and then I did so only on Margaret's insistence. I was beyond frightened. I was terrified. The day my appointment arrived, I thought my entire body was literally going to come apart and I'd be left picking pieces of myself up off the floor.

It didn't matter that the therapist had a kindly manner or that he possessed a non-threatening appearance. Nor did it matter that I really wanted to be there. My entire body was filled with fear and dread.

His opening question, "So, what brings you here today?"

sent shock waves through my body. How could I admit to anyone, let alone a stranger, what I knew to be true? That I was slipping away.

"I don't know," I managed to mumble. "Something is really wrong with my life."

If his first question sent shock waves through me, his second question caused generalized pandemonium. "Do you know what that might be?"

I stared out his office window. The air instantly became oppressive. I had the fleeting thought that maybe if I turned this whole session into a social visit maybe the pressure would ease up.

"You know, you've got quite a view of Los Angeles from up here when there isn't any smog. You're so high up."

He nodded his head. "Why don't you tell me a little bit about what's going on in your life, Anne?"

I swallowed hard and forced myself to turn back to the therapist. "Well, I'm very embarrassed by my present situation."

"In what way?"

"Hmm . . . see, I think people should be able to handle their own problems, manage their own lives." I shrugged my shoulders and smiled. "Apparently I can't do that anymore."

"What makes you think you can't handle your own life?"

"Because I cry all the time." I gazed around his office.

The deep mahogany bookshelves lining his office walls were beautiful. "Some days it gets so bad I actually think I'm going crazy. Boy, you sure have a lot of books here. Have you read every single one?"

"Most of them. Tell me what you mean by going crazy?"

"Crazy? Well . . . " Click. Suddenly I felt click. Something had just re-routed itself inside my body.

"Look," I announced with unexpected boldness, "I don't think I want to be married anymore. But I don't know what to do because the church says divorce is wrong and everything in my head is getting all messed up." My eyes filled up with tears. "There, I said it. I hope you don't think anything less of me because I've started to cry. I promised myself I wasn't going to let that happen today."

"Why did you feel you had to make that promise to yourself?"

"What do you mean why? Because crying is a terrible sign of weakness. Don't you agree?"

"Not necessarily."

I waited for him to say something more, but he didn't.

"Anyway, as I was saying. I can't seem to figure anything out anymore and I sure wish I could. Because if I could, then I wouldn't need you."

"Ah, yes. But if everyone could figure out their own problems, then I'd be out of a job, wouldn't I?"

The hour passed quickly and as the session drew to a close, he handed me a lengthy test. "I'd like you to fill this out before you return for your next visit."

"What is it?"

"It's called the Minnesota Multiphasic."

"Well, I'm from Minnesota and I've never heard of this test before."

"Really? It's used quite a bit."

"It's awfully long." I flipped through the pages. "I don't think I'll have time to do it."

"Try to do as much as you can. Tell me something, Anne. Does your husband know you're here today?"

"No! He's very fundamental in his beliefs and a wonderful Christian. He doesn't believe in psychiatrists and stuff. He thinks they're Satanic."

"He thinks I'm Satanic?" The therapist looked surprised.

"Well, maybe not you personally. I don't know. It just that Fundamentalists believe that anyone who helps you with your problems, unless he's a minister, of course, is probably from Satan."

"Only a minister can help?"

"Yes. Why are you acting like this doesn't make any sense? It makes perfect sense.

If you have a concern or need, you pray about it and God will answer your prayers. If you go to someone else to help you, you're not trusting God's spirit to help you. You're trusting in an earthly person, someone with skin on. And then, once you've done that, you've opened the door for Satan to influence you through the teachings of other people."

"Do you think I'm Satanic?"

"No. I mean, how could you be when my friend Margaret recommended you?"

"I guess that's somewhat reassuring. Regardless of what your husband does or does not believe about me, he needs to know you've made a decision to get some help, Anne. Keeping it a secret would only further undermine your marriage."

Again I found myself staring out the window. "I wish he'd never have to find out."

That evening at dinnertime I reached into the refrigerator for a carton of milk. "I saw a marriage counselor this afternoon," I said with a false calm that belied my pounding heart. "I'd sort of like to keep going. I think he can help us."

Bob's explosion was instantaneous. "You did what?"

The carton of milk slid through my hands and spilled out

into a large pool of liquid on the kitchen floor. Grabbing a sponge from the sink, I dropped down to my knees.

"You saw a what this afternoon?"

"A marriage counselor." The milk was running everywhere.

"Do you honestly think you can get me to believe that? We don't have enough money for you to do that, unless, of course, you're really having an affair and you think I'm stupid enough to buy this marriage counselor business."

I placed the empty milk carton in the trash.

"I'm not having an affair! Look, Bob, all I do is cry. We need, actually it's me—I need some help. I've decided to go to a psychologist to get that help. I'm sorry if you don't believe me, because it's the truth."

"How did you find this so-called marriage counselor?"

"Margaret referred me to him."

"Of course. I should have known. Your Bible Study teacher."

"I like Margaret! She's been a big help to me. And yes, she is my Bible study teacher. So, what!"

"Alright, Anne, let me make this perfectly clear. Even if this is a doctor you're seeing, I will not help you. I won't give you extra money to pay him. I'm not going to take care of the girls so you can keep your appointments. I won't even put gas in your car. Let's just see how long this little plan you and Margaret have cooked up lasts once you have to start working extra shifts to pay for everything. And, if I ever find out that this doctor business is a lie, you can forget about ever seeing the girls again."

I accepted his terms. There wasn't really any other choice.

An uneasy truce settled over the house. Bob had his schedule at the church. I had mine at the hospital and with the girls.

I still maintained my normal routine at Bob's church. Every Thursday night I sang at choir rehearsal and every Sunday morning I sang at all three morning services. Financially, emotionally and psychologically Bob needed to keep this job. We still appeared very much together, although at home I was already sleeping in the spare room that doubled as a utility room.

Bob thought the move from the bedroom was one more indication that Satan was using therapy as a way to split us up. "I'm praying for you," he told me the first night we slept apart. "God will bring you to your senses soon. I know He will."

Publicly he played the role of the loving husband and adoring father. He cultivated the congregation's praise and affections, and they returned his efforts with growing adoration.

So great was their outpouring of love that at one point one of the members stopped me on the street one day and said, "You must know that some people around here think your husband can walk on water."

To this comment and others like it, I smiled and said, "I appreciate your telling me that. Thank you." Bob's magic was working all over again. I'd heard and seen it all before. I was nineteen years old when he'd used it on me.

Privately, Bob continued to taunt me about my therapy appointments and the extra shifts I had to work to cover the cost of the therapy bills. I forced myself not to care. Therapy and the girls were all that mattered to me anymore. The fact that therapy left me more confused than ever did not sway me from my hope that God was at work in the process.

• • •

"That's it," the therapist asked with a quizzical look on his face. "That's all you can say? I ask you to describe your relationship with your father and all you can say is that he's 'a real snappy dresser?'"

"Look," I said more frustrated than mad, "I don't even want to talk about him at all. You're the one that keeps bringing him up. I was told to always keep my mouth shut about the family. And personally, I don't see how any of this is going to help me anyway. I came here to figure out what's going on with my marriage, not to talk about my father. I haven't seen my father in at least ten years and don't intend to see him anytime soon."

"Anne, do you remember all those diagnostic tests I gave you when you first came here?"

"Yes."

"Well, the results of those tests show you have some issues with your father that might need some work."

"I can't believe you actually put any stock in those stupid tests! I know I certainly didn't."

"Why don't you tell me a little more about this real snappy dresser and maybe we'll get some answers as to why you picked your husband in the first place."

I shook my head in disbelief. "Fine then, I'll tell you. But I fail to see how any of this is going to help."

"Okay. Well, first of all, it wasn't just that my father looked good; he looked like he could have stepped out of the pages of *Esquire* magazine. Now how he did that I'll never know because we were dirt poor most of the years I was growing up. Maybe he spent what money he did have on clothes. I don't know. And another thing—"

Quite unexpectedly, sorrow washed over me in a surprising flood of grief. Something had ripped through the fortress walls of my defenses.

My chin quivered as I struggled to find the words. "Actually, my dad . . . Well, let's just say my dad is one of the greatest disappointments I've ever had."

The room became very still.

"In what way did he disappoint you?"

I took a moment and cleared my throat. "Well, people always looked at him and thought he was this extraordinary person because he was this war hero and everything. He looked so good. You know? It took me the longest time to reconcile this public person that everybody else saw with the private person that lived at my house."

"And what was the private person like?"

Grief overcame me. "Do you think this is really going to help?" I sobbed. "I think my life has already been bad enough. If I talk about my dad it will only get worse. I've never talked about my dad to anyone."

"Maybe it's time you started."

I stared out the window for several seconds before turning back to the therapist.

"Well, okay, but I don't want you to make a big deal about this and I certainly don't want you to tell anyone. Promise? You need to understand that I'm not going to say one word until you promise."

The therapist nodded his head yes.

"You know, this nodding-of-your-head-business is fine, but I really need to hear you say something."

"I promise."

"Great. Then here's the deal. I'll tell you one thing about my dad this week and then we can go onto something else.

Next week I'll tell you one more thing about him and that's how it's going to go."

The therapist said nothing.

"My dad is totally messed up when it comes to sex," I said after an eternity of silence. "I hate to say that, but it happens to be the truth."

I paused searching for an example. "For instance, once I got back from a trip to Europe and my dad went berserk because my mother told him I'd given a boyfriend a kiss in public. I swear to you it was just a little itty-bitty kiss, but once he found out about it, he went ballistic. He said he couldn't believe that his very own goddamn daughter didn't know how to act at an airport. When I started to cry and carry on about how he wasn't being fair, he smacked me across the face. He hit me so hard he split my lip and gave me a black eye. Well, I gave up right then and there trying to make sense of anything with him. I didn't see much of him after that. Didn't talk to him much, either. If he wanted to say anything to me, which wasn't often, he sent messages through my mother. So that's the story for this week. Now can we get back to my marriage? Because like I said before, I honestly don't see how talking about my dad is going to help me right now. But a deal is a deal and next week I promise I'll tell you something else. Okay?"

"How do you feel now that you've told me something about your father?"

"I feel alright. I don't feel great. But then, I never feel great about anything."

"Do you trust me not to tell anyone?"

"Yeah, sort of."

"Is there anything I can do to reassure that I won't?"

"No. I guess only time will tell."

"Anne, you can trust me."

"Well, I sure hope you're right." I blew my nose and struggled to smile.

Rather than making my life better, as I had hoped, therapy began making things worse. It wasn't that my sessions didn't go well. They went very well.

The therapist listened attentively to what I had to say and my spirits lifted during the hour, but even before the session was over my emotional descent had begun. And yet, I still kept going.

I thought the therapist held the key to unlock the door of my mental confusion. I was positive that if I kept going and kept talking, one day I would wake up and the fog would have lifted. It never occurred to me to tell the therapist how discouraged I was getting. Not once.

All of my life I had been trained to take care of others. That was my job. And even if the therapy wasn't going very well, it was still my job.

During one isolated moment of courage, I did dare to ask the therapist a question. "Do you realize that all we ever talk about is my father? You've never even asked me about my mom. I don't think those tests can be very good if they don't at least show I have some problems with my mother."

"Would you like to talk about your mother today?"

I reached into my purse and pulled out a long slip of paper. "Yes. Yes, I would. As a matter of fact, I've brought in a list of things of I'd like to go over."

The therapist smiled. "That's quite a list you've got there. You seem to know where you're going with all of this, so why don't you just continue."

Energy surged through my body for the first time in months. "Okay, I will."

"For openers, this is a list of all the things my mother doesn't like. Let me be more specific. This is a list of things my mother doesn't like about me. These are not just things I imagined, okay? These are actual things she told me. "

The therapist nodded.

"You know, you really are gifted in this area of nodding. Anyway, about my list. First, she always thought I was a slow writer. Whenever I wrote a school paper, she'd harp about how long it took me. 'Anne,' she'd say, 'are you still working on that? Boy, you sure do write slow.' Eventually, it didn't make any difference what I was writing. It could have been my name for all it mattered and she'd have some mean comment to make about it. It got so bad that, after awhile, every time I went to pick up a pen my hand would start to shake. Now, as for number two . . . wait a minute I feel like I'm going to cry. I need to stop for a second."

"Take as long as you need."

I turned and stared out the window. "Okay, I'm better," I said looking back at the therapist. "I can go on. Now for number two . . . she always hated it when I tore my clothes. It's not like I meant to do it or anything. It just happened while I was playing."

"What would she do?"

"When?"

"When you tore your clothes?"

"She'd hit me. One time when I tore my good winter coat she got so mad she beat me until I had a bloody nose. Which brings me to number three. When I was little I used to get bloody noses a lot and it drove her crazy. Whenever I got one? Bam! She'd hit me again. It wasn't like I was black and blue or anything. So don't go getting the wrong impression, here. And, there wasn't one thing I could do as well as my sisters.

Not one! Man, that used to tick me off. They were prettier, thinner, smarter. They sewed better—she even said they were better babysitters than I was! And I knew that wasn't true because all the neighbors used to tell me how good I was!"

"Anne, I need to interrupt here. I don't think we're going to get through your list today."

"What do you mean? Do you need me to go faster?"

"No. We need to slow down and take a look at some of these things your mother did."

"No! I don't want to slow down. I just want to get through this list and be done with it."

Speed was of the essence. I didn't want to stop and discuss anything. I thought I could escape betraying the family by not going into detail. In my mind, being aware of what was on the list was not the same thing as really knowing. The distinction was a critical. In making the distinction, I had created a safety zone for myself. The therapist might know something but he didn't know everything. I may have talked, but I had not fully cooperated with the enemy. The sanctity of our family would still be intact.

"You'll never be done with it if we don't slow down and talk about some of these things. You'll carry this list around with you for the rest of your life."

We'd only made it to number three. I looked down at the paper and started to cry. My mother hated me and I didn't know why. *Somehow,* I'd thought, *if I can just make it through this list then everything would be all right.*

"I still have this whole list of stuff we didn't get to and now you tell me I'm going to carry this list around with me the rest of my life. This is awful . . . really awful."

"Anne, we can deal with everything that's on your list but not all at one time."

"Why not?"

"Because it's too much and it's too sad."

"Too sad?"

"Well, don't you think these stories you've told me about your mother are sad?"

"I've never thought about it being sad before. It seems like I've spent so much time trying to figure out why she didn't like me, I've never really thought about anything else. What am I going to do now?"

"For now, why don't you put your list away and let's talk about the reason you thought you came to see me in the first place."

"Why was that? I can't think right now. Oh . . . right. My marriage." And that's when I began to sob.

CHAPTER SIXTEEN

I Have God and the Whole Church on My Side

I hated talking to the therapist about my parents. Everything about them made me cry, and lately I'd been crying all the time. Within weeks, guilt and shame laid waste to the last vestige of my sanity and turned my mind into a battlefield. I was surprised to find talking about my parents so upsetting because I hadn't spoken to either one of them in years. That all changed with one phone call on a cool fall evening four months after my first session.

"Anne, this is your mother." Ancient alarm bells from deep inside my head started to clang.

"Your older sister just called and told me the most amazing thing. She said you were seeing a psychiatrist. Of course, I told her that it couldn't possibly be true because I know you'd never go to a total stranger and talk about your personal problems. Why, I told her, 'Anne wouldn't need anyone's help, let alone a total stranger's.' Now, I'm right about this aren't I, Anne? You'd never go to one of those kinds of doctors, would you?"

Quite unexpectedly the pressure from my clenched teeth delivered a shot of searing pain up the side of my face and into my middle ear.

"No, mother, you're wrong," I said as I pressed on my ear in an attempt to relieve the pain. "I am going to one of those kinds of doctors, only he's a psychologist, not a psychiatrist."

She gasped. "Anne, I'm shocked! Why? Why, would you ever do such a thing? You know very well those kinds of doctors never help. All they want to do is get you to talk about things that should never leave the home in the first place."

"We talk about a lot of different things."

"Like what?" Panic and anger had crept into her voice.

"Nothing you have to worry about."

"Well, what does Bob think of all this? I just can't imagine that he would agree to such a thing."

"He doesn't agree with it, but quite honestly, I don't care what he thinks anymore."

"Of course you care what he thinks. He's your husband! Now you listen to me. You'd better come to your senses and realize that you are a married woman with two small children. Your rightful place in this world is beside your husband. I certainly never went running off to some doctor every time I had problems in my marriage. I solved them myself. And that's exactly what you should be doing."

"Mother, could we just end this conversation? I don't mean to be rude but I'm getting a terrible headache."

"All I'm trying to do is offer a little motherly advice and you tell me that I'm giving you a headache?"

"I didn't say that. All I meant was I'm not feeling very well right now."

"All right, Anne, but just remember there are other people to think about in this world besides yourself."

"I'm well aware of that, Mother."

I hung up the phone and slumped down onto the yellow vinyl kitchen chair. Suddenly, it felt like all the shades in the house were drawn, night had fallen, and the electricity had begun to fail. It was eight in the evening. The girls were in bed, Bob was at choir rehearsal, and for the first time since I'd started therapy I made a decision to call the therapist for help.

The answering service picked up my message and within thirty minutes the therapist was on the line.

"Hi, Anne, the answering service said you called. Is there a problem?"

"I don't know."

"Did something happen?"

"No. Well . . . I just had a phone conversation with my mother and . . . I don't know. It was upsetting, I guess. That's all."

"What did she say that upset you?"

"Nothing really. My older sister had told her I was in therapy and she wasn't happy about it."

"Anne, I hate to rush you but I told my wife I'd be home an hour ago. Do you think this can wait until your appointment on Thursday?"

"Oh . . . sure . . . I guess it can wait."

"Unless, of course, there's something about this phone call you haven't told me."

"No, no. I'll see you on Thursday."

I hung up the phone. My mind was on fire and the pain in my chest was so intense I could hardly breathe. I started pacing back forth over the kitchen floor. Somehow I had to figure out a way to get this pain to stop. And then like a bolt of lightning it hit me. A plan! I'd thought of a plan. My body was awash in relief. The pressure had come off. The fog had lifted. I'd found a plan. And with the plan came an acceptable way to die.

Mentally I walked through the steps with barely any hesitation. First, I'd call one of the doctors at work and tell him I needed a prescription for sleeping pills. He already knew it'd been rough for me lately and besides, I'd tell him I only needed them for a couple of months. Then tomorrow after I dropped the girls off at school, instead of going to work, I'd leave my car in a parking lot and walk to the bus line.

After that I'd get on the first bus that came by and get off when I saw a motel. I'd check into motel, take the entire bottle of sleeping pills and lay down on the bed, then go to sleep. No one would be able to find me until it's too late. There'd be no humiliating divorce. Bob and the Church could raise the girls.

I wouldn't have to talk anymore about my mother and father to a therapist who had to be "home an hour ago." And my mother wouldn't have to deal with the embarrassment of having one of her children divorced.

For the first time in months everything was so clear. I picked up the phone to call the doctor for the prescription, but my fingers felt as if they were glued together. I simply couldn't get them to work. For several seconds I stared at phone and then tried again. Again my fingers refused to work. I continued staring at the phone and then eventually stared at nothing at all. The sound of the rapid busy signal from the receiver mesmerized me. Even the recorded message "If you'd like to make a call . . . " failed to get me to put the receiver back on the hook.

The pain in my chest reappeared and once again my mind started to race. I didn't really want to die. I only wanted the pain to stop. I sat down, put the receiver in my lap, covered my face with my hands, and rocked back and forth. What if I stayed in therapy, got my coping skills back, and survived all of this. Wouldn't a live mother—even a divorced one—be better for the girls than a dead one?

"I'm so confused," I cried out in agony.

Then, in the evening stillness, I heard a voice inside my head. "Give the therapist six more weeks."

I didn't move. I listened to every creak and groan in our tiny three bedroom house. I watched the clock on the kitchen stove and stared at the minute hand on my watch. The seconds turned into minutes.

The minutes turned into an hour. The pain in my chest began to ease up. Finally, I could take breath without an exquisite pain ripping through my chest. I got up from the chair. *Okay,* I thought. *I'll give the therapist six more weeks.*

I never understood where the six more weeks came from or why it wasn't five weeks or even four. But nothing in my life made sense anymore. This was just one more thing. I put the phone back on the hook and went to bed. I'd struck a bargain for my life. But as I walked back to my bedroom, I knew that six more weeks was all I was willing to give.

By the time Bob returned home I was already asleep.

Thursday arrived, and with it came my usual therapy appointment. It was the therapist who spoke first.

"Anne, I'd like to apologize for rushing you on the phone the other night. You've never called me for anything other than an appointment and I think that there was probably something more going on than just a phone call from your mother. I usually try to get home by a certain time and sometimes I use poor judgment when I return phone calls from the office. I'm sorry about not being there for you when you clearly had something bothering you."

His apology stunned me and made me feel uncomfortable. No one had ever apologized to me before. I didn't know what to say. I couldn't look at the therapist.

"You've changed the office chairs around," I said glancing around the office. "I usually sit in that tweedy thing you're in and you usually sit in the one I'm in."

"Yes. Yes, I did."

"I'm finding it kind of hard to talk now that you've gone and changed everything."

"Would you like me to move the chairs back?"

"No!" My voice cracked. "I'll be okay with it this way. Change is just weird for me. Umm . . . thank you for apologizing. I can't remember anyone doing that for me before."

"Anne, I think we need to spend some time on how you ask for help."

"I don't like to ask for help."

"I know that. But can we think about this for a moment? Is there anyone you can think of who didn't help you when you needed it? Or, did you ask for help from someone and not get it?"

"Yes! Of course there is," I shouted. "You know there is! But I can't go on talking about my parents any longer. There is far too much pain connected to them. Besides, I don't think talking about them is helping me one bit."

He said nothing in response as I reached for a tissue on the glass-topped coffee table. "I'm sorry I yelled. It's just that this is all so hard and quite honestly, I can't remember one single specific time I asked my parents for help. But I must have, because everybody asks for help at sometime, right? All I know is that I always had to figure everything out on my own. I started cleaning the house and doing laundry when I was seven. Now, how was I supposed to know anything about doing laundry at that age? Can you answer me that?"

Again he said nothing.

"See, you don't have anything to say, do you?" I tried to keep from crying but it was useless. Tears of anger and frustration overwhelmed me. "Well, if you ask me, I don't think you can make one thing about my parents any better. I don't think anybody can because nobody can change what happened. It just happened. That's all. Now I'm not going to say one more thing about my parents today. In fact, there's a chance I may never talk about them again for as long as I live."

I leaned over and grabbed the entire box of tissues. "Well, there is one more thing I'd like to say and then I swear that's it! Okay, here it is. There's a part of me that really hates them, and that's a hard feeling to have. I'm done now. I'm not going to talk anymore about my parents."

"That's fine, Anne. But I'd like it if you to tried to answer one more question."

"Maybe I will and maybe I won't."

"Do you have any happy memories from your childhood?"

"Nope," I fired back. "Oh, wait a minute, I do. I got a red bike when I was five. It was a boy's bike and a used one at that, but I still thought it was pretty spiffy. So I guess you could say that was a happy memory. But, then again, and here's where I get confused. I had a really hard time figuring out how the brakes worked. And one day when I was riding down the hill in front of our house I looked up and saw lots of cars whizzing by on the highway below. I didn't know how to stop the bike so I just ran it over a cement curb and flew headfirst over the handlebars. I woke up in the neighbor's house with this huge goose egg on my forehead and my mother standing over me with this odd look of satisfaction on her face. 'Well,' she said, 'you were the one that wanted the bike.' So I don't know. Maybe the bike wasn't such a happy memory after all."

"Were there times you felt that life was okay? Maybe not exactly happy, but okay?"

"I think things weren't too bad until I was five."

"What happened then?"

"Things just started getting weird and then we moved from the small town in southern Minnesota to Minneapolis."

"Do you know why you moved?"

"I think my dad had a business that failed, but I'm not sure. Anyway, everything changed after the move."

"What happened?"

"I can't remember. But it was bad."

"And you have no idea what it was?"

"Nope."

"Do you remember anything about that time at all?"

"Of course I do. I remember both my first and second grade teachers had black hair."

"Anything else?"

"Hey, do you think we can quit for today? I'm getting another one of my headaches and I'm feeling pretty pooped."

"Are you going to be okay?"

"Yeah, I just need a couple of Excedrin."

"Will you call me if you need to?"

"Maybe."

"I'd like it if you would."

"I don't know what I'll do. Right now I need some Excedrin. You know what you do at the end of each session? You smile at me. Did you know that?"

"I don't think I was aware of that. Maybe it's just because I like you."

"You do? Oh, that's nice."

I left the office and never mentioned the six-week time limit that was in play.

The atmosphere at home remained tense.

Bob believed God was on his side and he had nothing to worry about.

I believed God was working through the therapist and the therapist had five weeks left.

"Well," I announced to the therapist when the six weeks were up. "You're off the hook."

He looked surprised. "That's very nice to hear, but I didn't know I was on one."

"Oh, I know that," I said a little too brightly. "I didn't tell you because I didn't want you to worry. Do you remember when I phoned you late in the evening about six weeks ago and told you how upset I was with my mother? Well, things got so bad for me that night I figured the only way to get the pain to stop was to call it quits. I had it all planned out and everything. But then I changed my mind. I decided to give you one more chance."

"So, how am I doing?"

"Good." I smiled. "You're doing good."

"Do you know what made the difference for you?"

"I think your apology helped a lot. But mostly it was because of one afternoon a couple of weeks ago."

"What happened then?"

I told him how I'd had a day off and girls were at school, so I bought a Sidney Sheldon book and sat down on the sofa to read it. I'd been at it about thirty minutes when I suddenly realized I was just sitting there reading. I wasn't biting my fingernails, pulling my hair, or even picking at my lip—all the things I normally do when I try to read a book.

"I was just sitting there and reading like a normal person," I told him. "And for the first time in my entire life it felt okay to be wearing my own skin. It was such a weird feeling to have that I actually stood up and walked around the living room staring at my arms and legs. After I checked the time on the clock in the kitchen, I ran back to the sofa and assumed my exact same position and stayed there until the feeling went away. Once it was gone, I got up and checked the time again. Would you believe that only twenty minutes had passed? Now, I know twenty minutes doesn't seem like much and I can tell by the way you're smiling at me that you don't think it was very much either, but here's the deal. I figured if it happened once, it just might happen again. Only next time, with any kind of luck, it would last a little longer. So far there haven't been any more days like that one, but at least it's a start. So, what do you think?"

"About . . . "

"About my new feeling of wearing my own skin. You think it's stupid, right?"

"No, I don't think it's stupid at all. I was smiling at you because I've never had one of my patients time their feelings before and I'm very happy that you've experienced such a turnaround. However, let me also say that it makes me more than a little nervous for you to go through such a period of desperation all by yourself. If you ever become that desperate again I need you to call me, even if it's not during office hours. And I promise you, Anne, I'll be there for you. Together we're going to get you through this."

"Thanks. It's nice to hear you say that, but I'm not sure I believe you."

"You don't?" The therapist looked surprised.

"Did I just hurt your feelings? I didn't mean to if I did. You're okay aren't you?"

"I'm okay."

I breathed out a sigh of relief. "Good. I hate it when I accidentally hurt people's feelings. Now, could we move onto another topic?"

"If you'd like."

"Well, I know I don't have the courage to get a divorce just yet but I'm pretty sure I will someday, and I'd like to talk about how badly I feel about the girls."

"What about the girls?"

"I've always wanted them to come from a two parent home—not one."

"All your children need, Anne, is one parent who believes in them completely. Just one."

"Really? Just one?"

"Well, that's one more than you had. Isn't it?"

I wasn't sure I believed him but as I left the office that day it felt as if someone cared if I survived this marriage or not. The dark clouds which normally hovered two inches above my head were gone, and as I stepped into the elevator it occurred to me that for the second time in my life it felt good to be wearing my own skin.

Eighteen months of non-stop therapy later, I thought I was strong enough to tell Bob I wanted a divorce. But every time I opened up my mouth to say, "I want a divorce," the words got stuck somewhere between my throat and my tongue. I simply couldn't get my lips to form the words. And then, one morning in January, as I was pulling out a load of warm laundry from the dryer, I heard a voice inside my head say, "tell him now." I gathered the clothes into my arms and walked the short hallway to Bob's bedroom. I stood for a moment and watched as he got out of bed. "I'm going to file for a divorce in June," I blurted out. "That will give you six months to plan for whatever you need to do to live on your own and it'll give Kim a chance to finish her school year with the least amount of disruption."

There was no "I think we need to talk," no "there's something important I need to tell you," no "this is going to be very difficult, but I've come to a decision."

There was nothing except my decision to end the marriage and when I was going to do it.

I stood in the bedroom doorway and clung to the warm laundry like a child who clings to her favorite stuffed animal for security. I knew the laundry wasn't going to protect me from anything, but I found the heat coming off the clothes comforting and it gave me something to hang onto to stop my arms from shaking.

Bob rubbed the sleep from his eyes and threw back his head. "Divorce me," he scoffed. "Don't make me laugh. You'll never have the courage to divorce me, never in a million years."

Then he got up and walked down the hallway into the kitchen.

Still clutching the laundry, I followed him. "No, listen to me, I mean this. I want a divorce. I can't go on being married to you anymore. I feel like I'm dying."

He opened the refrigerator door, took out his habitual early morning Diet-Pepsi and turned to face me.

"So this is what you've been doing in therapy with your so-called doctor? Trying to figure a way out of the marriage? Well, if you ask me, I think you're worse off now than when you started all this therapy business. You cry all the time and complain about how bad your headaches are. What you need to do is pray and ask for God's help. If you did that, instead of going to this marriage counselor of yours, you'd see our marriage turn around. Quite frankly, Anne, I have to tell you I'm quite concerned about you. I'm going to tell the church that you want a divorce and that I'm totally against it. I'm also going to ask them to pray for you. Everything will change for the better. You'll see."

"No, I don't see." My voice shook and my chin quivered, but I carried on. "You can believe anything you want and I don't care how many people you get to pray for me. When June comes, I'm filing for divorce."

Years later, I wondered what it was about that morning that made me finally tell him what I was planning to do. I never really knew. Nothing had happened that morning that was anything out of the ordinary. So, I guess it was nothing. And it was everything.

• • •

The calls started coming from concerned church members almost immediately. Some were awkward. Some were blunt. All said the same thing. "Bob loves you and the girls so much. Please try to work this out. Divorce is such a terrible thing." All of them ended kindly. "I just want you to know we're praying for you."

My response was always the same. "Thank you for calling. I appreciate your concern." Their concern, however, didn't stop with phone calls.

During a casual conversation at work, one of the staff doctors mentioned to me that prayer meetings were now being held at the church on my behalf.

The congregation had now joined together to corporately

petition God to get me to change my mind. When I asked him how he knew this, his response shocked me.

"Oh, my mother goes to that church."

"Your mother knows my husband?"

"Not personally, no. But, apparently your husband shares a great deal of his personal life with the congregation. You looked surprised. I'm sorry. I thought you knew."

"No, I didn't."

As soon as the girls left for school the following morning I confronted Bob.

"What are you telling people at church about me?"

"What are you talking about?"

I told him what I'd heard. "And I want to know what you're saying."

"You knew that I was going to tell the church that you wanted a divorce. I don't know why you're acting so surprised."

"The whole church? You had to tell the whole church?"

"Yes, I had to tell the whole church. We need all the prayer we can get."

"What else have you said?"

"That I was dead set against it."

"What else?"

"That's pretty much it. Why are you so upset about this? The only thing I want to do is to save our marriage, and if the congregation is willing to pray for us then I want them to do it."

"You are such a hypocrite! You don't care about our marriage. The only thing you care about is looking good in front of your precious congregation! Well, maybe I can't quote Scripture the way you can and maybe I really don't understand the Bible the way you do, but I know that God's going to get me through this even if I don't have a thousand people praying for me!"

"Are you done?" Bob asked with irritating calm.

"Yes."

"Then you need to know that tomorrow Pastor Welling is going to call you. I wanted him to talk to you and he agreed that it was a good idea."

"Is Pastor Welling your ultimate weapon?"

"You know, Annie, you don't seem to understand who the enemy really is. Satan is the enemy. Not me. He's the one that wants to take our marriage away from us. Pastor Welling is going to help you understand exactly what's at stake here."

"This may come as a big surprise to you, but I already know what's at stake here."

Pastor Welling was the senior pastor at Bob's church and he was the one person who single-handedly had the power to terminate Bob.

If Bob got divorced, the policy of the Baptist Denomination at that time dictated that he be fired. I had to try and convince Pastor Welling to go against the policy.

I dreaded his phone call. The next day, I jumped every time the phone rang. When it was a woman's voice, I thought it was another person from the congregation, but then she said, "This is Arlene, the pastor's secretary. Pastor Welling wanted me to call and set up a luncheon meeting with you this week. He has Wednesday afternoon at one o'clock free. Would that work for you?"

"Yes."

"There's a lovely restaurant not far from here called the Lautrec. I'll call you back with directions. Shall I assume this meeting is confirmed then?"

"Yes. Wednesday's fine."

I hung up the phone. How could I ever convince Pastor Welling to keep Bob on staff and at the same time tell him that even if he didn't, I was going to go ahead with the divorce? The anticipation of this meeting terrified me.

Fortunately for me, I liked Pastor Welling. He was not remarkable in stature or appearance, but he had a presence that comforted me. And even though he wore thick glasses, and occasionally could be quite stern, there was something about him that drew people to him. His congregation numbered in the thousands.

The interior of the restaurant he had selected was done entirely in dark green carpeting with peach floral tablecloths.

Healthy-looking green plants with polished leaves covered the main dining room and there was a small rock waterfall in the corner. It was, as Arlene had mentioned on the phone, lovely. Pastor Welling was already seated when I arrived, and as I approached the table, he stood up.

"Thank you for coming, Anne."

I nodded and smiled, but said nothing. I desperately wanted to get through this meeting without crying and immediately reached for the glass of water on the table as soon as I sat down.

The waiter handed us the menus. I knew the restaurant might be expensive, but was astonished to see that a simple tuna salad, which I loved, cost seven ninety-five.

"Anne, I asked for this meeting, so you're my guest. You were kind enough to come, so please don't pay any attention to the prices."

"Thank you. I was getting a little worried."

I ordered the tuna salad. He ordered the shrimp and explained a bit apologetically, "I seldom order the shrimp, but in my line of work you eat an awful lot of chicken. I thought I would treat myself to something different today."

As soon as we ordered lunch, he wasted no time in getting to the point. "Anne, you need to know that if you go through with this divorce, your husband is going to lose his job."

My hands were clasped so tightly under the table they started to ache. Even so, I kept a gaze on him and replied, "Ever since I decided to file, I've dreaded hearing those words from you."

"With the exception of adultery and abandonment, the Bible forbids divorce," Pastor Welling continued, "and the Baptists are a Bible-believing people. We don't believe in having divorced or separated members on our staff. We made an exception in Bob's case because he assured us that his first marriage had ended only because of his ex-wife's adulterous affair. But we will not make another."

I nodded my head but said nothing about how Bob had pursued me while he was still married. I was obsessed with my goal. My children needed a father. Their father needed a job. Any secrets I had about Bob's behavior which would prevent that from happening were going to remain exactly that —secrets.

Conversation temporarily stopped when the waiter arrived with our food.

"Would you like to ask God to bless our food, Anne?"

"I can't. I'm sorry. I'm too nervous."

We bowed our head as Pastor Welling gave a sweet, simple blessing. "Thank you, Father, for Anne and her willingness to be here. And, may you bless the food we eat and the words we speak today."

The tuna salad that had sounded so inviting, now suddenly looked unappealing. I started to pick at it and hoped that Pastor Welling, who had enthusiastically attacked his salad, hadn't noticed.

He focused on his food for a short time and then put his fork down and looked at me. "Now tell me. Are you absolutely committed to going through with this?"

"Yes. I am."

He nodded. "Very well. Then I want you to think some things through with me. Are you aware that almost the entire congregation is on your husband's side? That means you'll have very little support once you're on your own."

I pushed the food around on my plate. "I have some support, through the Bible Study I've been attending at another church."

"Yes, I suppose you do. But Anne, you need to understand you're going to be alone. You'll have to work full-time and take care of the children. They're still very small. You'll not have one free moment from responsibility. You'll be exhausted."

"Pastor Welling, I don't mean you any disrespect, but you really don't know me, and there's a lot you don't know about my marriage. For one thing I was born tired. So being exhausted isn't going to be much worse. And for another, I am going to get a divorce. I don't want to go on living if I have to be married to Bob. I know divorce goes against what the Bible teaches. Honestly, I do. But, I just can't believe God wants me to go on living like this. He just can't."

There. I'd done it. I'd told him I wanted a divorce and I hadn't cried. I'd come close a couple of times, but I hadn't fallen apart. Oddly enough, the longer I went on talking the stronger I felt.

"Bob has this fabulous public image that people fall for. They think he's a terrific father and loving husband because he tells everybody how much he loves us. Well, he's a marginal parent at best and he cares more about his career than he could ever possibly care about the girls or me. He loves us. I know that. But his ambition to be famous comes first and it's killing us."

If Pastor Welling was surprised by what I was saying, he did not indicate it. In fact, he gave very little reaction at all. He just sat there listening, the rest of his salad uneaten.

I went on. "I know that I technically don't have Biblical grounds. But I feel like I'm dying. I've often thought I should go to the Red Cross and ask for all the transfusions I can get because it feels like I don't have any blood left in my body. And even though everything I've told you is true, I know Bob's going to be lost without me. He's not going to know how to live his life. I just know it. If you take his job away from him he'll fall apart. Then I'll have to take care of everybody, Bob included, and the girls will end up with no father at all. I realize that you don't allow divorced people on your staff, but I'm pleading with you to make an exception. If not for Bob then do it for the girls and me. I need him to keep his job. My children need him to keep his job."

I'd run out of words. I looked at Pastor Welling and waited. When he finally spoke his voice was filled with tenderness.

"Anne, I know a great deal more than you think I know. Over time, I've watched you with your children and I want you to know that both you and your girls mean a great deal to me. I'm sorry I was so hard on you today, but I needed to find out how committed you were to proceeding with the divorce. Now that I realize you're not going to change your mind, I guess the one thing that would help you the most is to keep Bob on staff. You understand that our church will have to answer to the head of the denomination for our decision to go against church policy. But I think I'll be able to prevail."

"However," he added, "it's my belief that you're going to have an extremely difficult time of things and nothing, I'm afraid, can change that. If it's any consolation, I'd like you to know that even though I'll never come out publicly and say so, you have my complete support as well as my wife's."

Then he lightly patted my hand and said "God bless you, Anne," as he picked up the check and left.

Except for Sunday mornings in the pulpit, I never saw Pastor Welling again. Nor did I ever find out if he had to defend his actions to the head of the denomination.

But when I filed for divorce not only did he keep Bob on staff, he provided a small house for him to live in rent free until he was able make the transition on his own. Pastor Welling had quietly saved my life and for that I was grateful. It did not matter to me that I had no place left in his church. Neither did it matter that no one called me anymore. The only thing that mattered to me was that Bob had a job and that my children still had a father.

CHAPTER SEVENTEEN

Disaster Caught Me Unaware

"Well," Bob said with a smug look of anticipation when I walked through the door.

I hung up my jacket in the front closet. "Well, what?"

"Well, I hope you understand that if you go ahead with these plans of yours, I'll lose my job."

I didn't want to look at him anymore. I didn't even want to hear his voice. "You won't lose your job," I said as I headed towards the bedroom. "I need to change into my uniform. I have to get ready for work."

Halfway down the hallway Bob grabbed me by the arm and pinned me up against the wall. "Of course I'm going to lose my job! They've never had one single person in the history of that church that's ever gotten divorced and remained on staff! Can't you see you're going to ruin me?"

My hand started to tingle from lack of circulation, but the meeting with Pastor Welling had strengthened my resolve.

Bob's power to keep me caged up in this marriage was

over. The air around me was filled with the sweet, intoxicating scent of freedom.

I glared at him. "I'm not the one that's going to ruin you. You're ruining yourself. Now, will you please let go of my arm? You're hurting me."

Our eyes locked on to each other in mutual defiance. Seconds ticked away.

Finally, he released his grip. "Annie, please, you've got to listen to me. I didn't want to tell you like this, but I have a surprise for you. Someone from the church has offered to help us buy a big ranch-style house not far from here. I've already been through it and it's perfect for us. It's so big that I could live at one end of the house and you and the girls could live at the other. You wouldn't even have to see me if you didn't want to. We could get this house and still be together as a family. Don't you see? It's the perfect solution!"

I rubbed my hand and tried to ease the pain. "Let me see if I have this straight. You think a bigger house will solve all our problems?"

"Yes, I do. If we had a bigger house we wouldn't feel so confined. The girls would have room to play . . . "

"Hold it right there. Since when did you ever care about how much room the girls had to play in? And what about me? Am I just supposed to take up residence at one end of the house and act like we're still married? What kind of life is that for me? I'll tell you what kind of life that is; it's no life! So no, I won't go see the house. And no, I won't even think about it. Now get out of my way so I can get ready for work. I have to be at the hospital in an hour and I don't want to be late."

His eyes hardened. "I can't believe you won't even consider my proposal."

"Well, believe it. Because I won't." I pushed him aside and went into the bedroom to change.

When I returned to the living room to get my sweater and purse, Bob was sitting at the dining room table with his head in his hands.

"You promised that if I met with Pastor Welling today you'd pick up the girls from school and take care of them tonight, remember?"

He glared at me, and then silently got up from the table, walked into the kitchen, and picked up his car keys. He turned around at the front door. "If you think that by filing for a divorce you can get me to move out of my house or take my girls away from me, you'd better think again. I love you too much to let you go. We can still be together and you'll be able to live your own life if we move to a bigger house. But if you won't do it, and let me make this perfectly clear, I will take you to court and I will get the girls. I have the support of the entire congregation. You've spent so much time working that I don't think I'll have any trouble getting the judge to see you as the unfit mother you really are. There are lots of influential people in the church who think you're dead wrong on this and I'm sure they'd be willing to testify on my behalf. So I suggest you think about what you're doing a little longer." He didn't bother to shut the door on his way out.

My newly discovered resolve collapsed under the crush of his words. I reached into my purse for my car keys.

Just stay calm, Anne. Stay calm. He's not going to take the girls from you. He's not. He's just trying to scare you. You're not an unfit mother just because you have to work. Don't panic. You've got to get through another eight hours at the hospital.

I locked the front door, climbed into my car and headed onto the freeway. *Breathe, Anne, keep breathing. Everything's going to work out fine. Bob will never start a custody fight for the girls. So what if he says he has God and the whole church on his side? No judge would let him have the girls just because of that. Would he?*

Bob may have wanted God to save his marriage, but there was no doubt in my mind that he was now ready to do combat for the girls. His words had taken aim and hit their mark. I was now terrified.

I'd never experienced a nightmare before, but that night my walk through the valley of nighttime terrors announced itself with an awesome ferocity.

> *It is wintertime in Nazi Germany. I'm fifteen and seated next to the window on a wartime train with my father. I watch mile after mile of the snow-covered, sun-filled countryside speed by the window. The passengers are dressed in smart winter clothing. The Nazi soldiers are in uniform. Many are smoking. We've been told that we're going to a celebration and I've worn my best burgundy dress coat trimmed with black velveteen on the collar and cuffs.*
>
> *Sitting next to my father I'm convinced that he's the best-looking man on the train and his decorated Army uniform only adds to my feeling of pride.*
>
> *As the train rolls on, several of the German soldiers begin to stare at me and whisper amongst themselves. Finally, one of them leans over and says to my father. "She's not one of us. She cannot be trusted. She will talk. You must get rid of her."*
>
> *My father turns to stare out the window but says nothing.*
>
> *The train rolls on through the snow-filled countryside.*
>
> *The soldiers frighten me. "Please tell them I can be trusted," I plead with my father. "Tell them I won't say anything."*

My father remains silent as my agitation grows. "Please, you've got to say something! I think they're going to kill me. They think I'm going to talk. Tell them I can be trusted."

The soldiers stare at me and then stare at my father. Still he says nothing.

No one speaks as the monotonous rhythmic clacking of the train takes us to our final destination. A soldier lights up a cigarette.

The train slows down as it approaches the celebration site. My father turns to the soldiers and says, "You can trust her. She's been sent as a substitute for Anna." Then he turns to me. "They don't want to kill you. They only want to take your picture." He pauses slightly before leaning over to whisper in my ear, "When they raise their cameras, run."

The train stops. The happy unsuspecting passengers get off and proceed to the entrance of the covered bridge where their picture will be taken to mark the occasion. My father waves to me as I exit the train.

I panic when I realize he isn't getting off the train and start running back through the crowd of people making their way up to the celebration site. "Why aren't you getting off?" I yell in desperation as the engines start up.

I look up. I see him mouth the word, "Run."

I am swallowed up in the crowd and can't break free without drawing attention to myself.

At a designated spot everyone is told to get into lines with the tallest in back. Once everyone is in position they turn to smile at the cameras. But it is already too late.

The cameras have turned into rifles and the sound of gunfire shatters the quiet of the countryside.

I'm already running when people around me begin to

crumple. The moaning of the dying and bullets flying forces me to run harder, and with each step I run, I get younger and younger. By the time I find safety in a nearby gazebo I am no longer fifteen. I am six years old and because I am now small, my body fits neatly into a crawl space beneath a wall bench covered with sliding white latticework. The Nazis enter the building just as I pull the latticework in front of my face.

From my position I can see their knee-high boots advancing in my direction. My eyes grow wider and wider with each advancing step. For reasons that are not clear to me, confusion takes over the group. No one really knows if they saw me enter the building or not. "Let's go," someone says. "She's not worth all this trouble. She'll probably die of starvation or freeze to death, anyway." They laugh and talk to each other as they leave the building.

As their laughter fades into the distance, I inch my way out of my hiding place. I am alive—alive in a country at war and everyone around me is dead.

"Who," I wonder, "will help me now?"

I awoke with a start. My body was drenched in sweat. I gathered the blankets around me, hugged my knees to my chest and started to pray. "Please, God, please help me. I'm sweating, freezing and terrified. Bob's going to try and take the girls from me. I know he is. You've got to help me. I can't do this divorce all by myself. I can't. I'll make You proud of me, honest I will. The girls will turn out fine. You'll see. I promise. I promise. I promise."

My rocking continued and at some point I became aware of the fact that my rapidly pounding heart had started to slow down. I'd started to warm up.

"Okay, so somehow I think You heard me. I'm going to lie

down and all I need from You right now is one miracle. A big one. I need to get some sleep."

Wrapped in the fetal position, I lay down and rocked until the next thing I knew sunlight was streaming in through the window and Kim was standing two inches from my face. "Mommy," she whispered. "I don't want to be late for school."

I called the therapist later that morning and he returned my call almost immediately. "Hi, Anne, the answering service said you called. What's going on?"

"Is there a chance you could see me before our regular Thursday appointment? Like today?"

"You sound a little tense."

"I am. Do you have any time today?"

"You know, I'm completely booked. But if this is an emergency I can try and switch some time slots around."

"No, it's not an emergency. I just don't think I can wait until the end of the week."

"Can you come in at ten tomorrow?"

"Yes!"

"Are you sure there's nothing you can tell me now?"

"I had a dream, nightmare actually, and I don't know how to deal with it. That's all."

"Okay, let's work on it tomorrow. Call me if you need to."

I hung up the phone and got through the next twenty-four hours one minute at a time.

I arrived much too early for my appointment the next day and knew I didn't look like someone who was once inch from falling apart. I had an ironclad rule: the worse I felt, the better I tried to look. Recently an article in *Glamour Magazine* said that short hair was going to be the next "in" thing and on a whim I'd cut off my shoulder length brown hair and dyed it auburn. Bob's reaction was immediate and intense. He hated it.

"How could you do this to me?" he yelled. "You know how much I loved your long hair."

I didn't care what he said. I was glad to be free of it at last.

If anything bothered me about my appearance, it was my weight. I could never find a good enough reason to eat and my weight had started into a steady decline. Most of my clothes now hung free on my five-foot ten-inch frame.

Lost in thought, I was startled when the therapist opened his office door.

"Come on in, Anne."

I got up from the chair and readjusted my skirt.

"You're looking well today," he said as I sat down in his office.

"Oh, thanks."

"So if you're ready why don't we get right into your dream."

In the safety of the therapist's office I was able to describe the dream with little difficulty.

"So who's Anna?" he asked when I'd finished.

"Anna?" I sank down into the chair.

"Yes. You said in the dream that you had been sent as a substitute for Anna. Do have any idea who that might be?"

I sank further into the chair and looked down at the floor.

"Anne, where are you right now?"

I raised my head and cleared my throat. "Here."

"You weren't a minute ago."

"I know, but I am now. I don't know who Anna is. I don't know anybody named Anna."

"Can you remember ever reading about someone named Anna that you closely identified with?"

I gazed down at my hands folded together in my lap. I was in a daze. It took tremendous energy to just listen to the therapist's question and try to come up with an answer. I simply wanted to float away. The therapist was looking at me with concern. I cleared my throat. "Only Anne Frank. Sometimes in the books I've read they refer to her as Anna as well as Anne."

"And what happened to Anne Frank?"

"The Nazi's found her family's hiding place and sent them all to concentration camps."

"Is there anything specific about her that stands out in your mind?"

"She couldn't live like a normal person at all. She had to live her life in hiding and if she left her hiding place, the Nazi's would kill her. I also know that some people believe her father betrayed her."

"How long have you been in hiding, Anne?"

Several seconds passed before I answered. "All my life."

The room became perfectly still. "I need to know if you feel safe right now before we continue."

"Yes." I picked at non-existent lint on the chair. "Right now I do."

"Then let's go back to the dream again. You start the dream when you're fifteen, but your age regresses once you start running. How old were you by the time you were hiding in the gazebo?"

"Six, I think. Why?"

"Because I think it's fairly safe to say that based on this dream something happened to you at the age of six that sent you into hiding."

"But I've already told you I can't remember anything that

happened to me then. How's going over it now going to help?"

"Well, I think in the context of the dream we'll have more to work with."

"Do you mind if we rest awhile? I can feel another one of my headaches starting. Maybe we can talk about something else or have a shorter session today."

"That's fine with me. But before we do, let me just point out something to you. This dream occurred after Bob threatened to sue for custody of the girls if you went through with the divorce. And I think you're going to feel more alone the closer it gets to the time that you actually file. Your nightmares may increase or you might actually begin to remember unpleasant events from the past as this divorce process goes forward."

"Why?"

"Because when you divorce you'll be on your own for the very first time in your life and you're going to feel quite vulnerable. I'd like you to make a commitment to me."

"Commitment? What kind of commitment."

"I want you to promise me that you will not harm yourself in any way, and that you will call me if you need me."

"Sure, I'll promise you that. But I think you're making a big deal about nothing. I mean, we're only talking about a dream here. Besides, if something really awful did happen, don't you think I'd remember it?"

"Not necessarily. Sometimes a person can block memories. It's sort of like putting them in a room somewhere and then closing the door."

"Can we move on to something else, now? My head is really starting to pound."

"Sure. Would you like to talk about the girls?"

And for the first time that day I smiled.

The dream continued to plague me. Why couldn't I remember why I'd gone into hiding? I asked myself that question over and over again but there was never any answer.

Time was moving on. It was already April and I needed to find an attorney. I asked my therapist for a referral, but his response was not very helpful.

"Why don't you ask some of your friends for some suggestions?"

"Because I don't have any divorced friends," I answered matter-of-factly. "Most of the women friends I had in the Bible Study never called me again after I told them I was going ahead with the divorce. I do have one friend in that group, but she couldn't help with anything legal."

"None of them called you?"

"Why do you look so surprised? It's very easy for people to support you as long as you never do anything wrong. I had to drop out of the group, anyway. I needed to work extra shifts to pay for lawyer's fees."

"Why don't you ask Margaret for a referral?'

"Margaret, my Bible Study teacher?"

"Now you're the one who's looking surprised. She might have a referral for you. After all, she referred you to me."

Fortunately for me, Margaret did have a suggestion and the attorney turned out to be much like Margaret herself: older, kind, wise and supportive. He was also willing to take payments on installments for his services.

I was so nervous during our first appointment I had to frequently ask him to repeat himself.

Somehow my intense anxiety had reduced my ability to comprehend even the simplest question to zero.

If the attorney was dismayed, he didn't indicate it. He

repeated what I didn't understand and graciously walked me to the door at the end of the hour. "As soon as you bring the information I need, I'll get the paperwork together."

I did not trust myself to speak. I simply nodded my head.

His smile was warm and caring as he opened the door. "I've been doing this for a very long time, Anne. I can get you through this."

Early in the afternoon I walked out of the attorney's office and late that night I walked into another nightmare.

My older sister, Sherry, is nine months pregnant and in labor. From the upstairs window, we can see the hospital on a hill not far from our childhood home, but we have no way to get there. We decide to walk, but Sherry doesn't want to leave just yet.

"Find Dad and tell him where I'm going."

I am annoyed by the request. "Why do you want me to try and find Dad? What difference does it make where he is? Let's just go."

But Sherry is insistent. "Just try will you, please? He needs to know I'm going to the hospital."

I make one phone call and give up. "I'm not spending any more time trying to find him. Let's just go."

We begin our walk to the hospital. In route, Jane, our younger sister, joins us. Sherry immediately begins to plead with her to go find Dad.

"I know where he is, so stop worrying," Jane tells Sherry. "When we get to the hospital, I'll call him."

The hospital turns out to be further than we'd thought and as Sherry's labor advances she begs and cries for frequent rests. Increasingly worried that we aren't going to make it to the hospital on time, I urge her onward.

It is sunrise. The road is deserted. The three of us press on.

We finally reach the hospital and Sherry is immediately taken to the delivery room.

Jane finds a telephone in the waiting room. Within minutes I hear her yelling. "You'd just better get here!" As she slams the phone down she turns to me. "I hate him," she says under her breath. "I really hate him!"

I do not react. I simply ask her one question. "Is he coming?"

My father appears just as the nurse arrives and is scanning the waiting room. "Sherry's just had a baby girl. Is the father here?"

I already know the answer and leave the waiting room to make my way down to the newborn nursery. As I'm leaving I hear my father say, "I'm the father."

The nurse assumes the question had been misunderstood. "No, what I meant was, is the baby's father here?"

Again my father answers. "I'm the father."

The nurse gives my father a cold stare and says, "Follow me."

Meanwhile, in the nursery, my greatest fear is confirmed. The baby looks just like my father and I decide to go ahead with my plan.

Stepping behind the curtain to hide, I reach into my purse and pull out a butcher knife.

Within a matter of seconds my father appears at the nursery with Jane, and the moment I hear the nurse say, "Here's your new daughter," I jump out from behind the curtain.

"You will never touch another little girl again," I hiss as I plunge the knife into my father's back and he falls to the floor.

I awoke from the dream in the early morning hours, eased myself out of bed and stood at the window to watch the sun spread its rays of first light upon the day. I didn't feel particularly disturbed. It felt as though the dream had been about another family, not mine. But during the week I started to notice things were starting to slip away. Dirty laundry piled up. Clean laundry sat in baskets on top of the washer and dryer, and even though fast foods had long since been a way of life, the dishes still somehow managed to accumulate on top of the counter. I looked around the house one morning before leaving for my regular Thursday therapy appointment and thought, *I think I'm going to start using paper plates. Dishes are too much trouble.* I had no idea as I closed the door on my disheveled home that day everything was going to turn out so badly. Had I known, I could've made other preparations. I might have asked my next-door neighbor Laura, to pick up the girls from school. Or even taken the day off. Or called in sick. But disaster caught me unaware.

Suicide hadn't entered my mind since the early days of therapy. Through personal study and Margaret's teachings in the Tuesday morning Bible Study, my confidence in God had grown daily. Her friendship and guidance both as a Bible teacher and friend had been a source of comfort and strength. And even though I'd been tremendously disappointed by the loss of friendship my divorce proceedings had caused, I never thought God had let me down.

I felt I was, at last, beginning to understand what God meant when He gave us free will. People could choose to be your friend—or not. I did not blame God for their abandonment. Nor did I blame God for the choices I had made in my life. The choices I'd made that had brought me great heartache and pain had also brought me great joy and delight.

But my losses were mounting and each loss was getting harder to bear.

I settled into my chair and smiled at the therapist. "Ready to go to work?"

"Anytime you are."

"I had another weird dream that involved my dad again. Only this time I'm pretty sure it was about sex."

"Sex?"

When the therapist repeated the word "sex" my hands started to shake. "Well, I'm not certain it was about sex. I only think it was. See, both of my sisters were there and Sherry was pregnant, and she wanted us to call Dad because it was supposed to be his baby and . . . "

"Anne, slow down. Slow down."

I couldn't slow down. My mouth was so dry my upper lip began sticking to my front teeth. "I don't know what's wrong with me. This dream didn't seem like such a big deal when I started into it, but right now it seems awful."

"Why don't we just start at the top and remember you're here now. You're safe. I've heard everything, I think, there is to hear. Nothing is going to shock me. So slow down and let's start over."

I tried to begin again, but my hands distracted me. I couldn't get them to stop shaking. Finally, I just sat on them. "What do you think this all means?" I asked as I finished telling him the dream still sitting on my hands.

The therapist emitted a deep sigh. "Let's go back to the first dream you told me about when you were six years old. Something happened that terrified you so badly that you went into hiding. Do you still have no idea what that might have been?"

My eyes filled with tears and I shook my head no.

"Okay. Let's go to the second dream. You said you left the hospital waiting room because you already knew the answer to the nurse's question. How did you know?"

I dropped my head and started to rock and weep.

The therapist gently pressed on. "Let's go on. Do you have any idea why all three of you girls appeared in the dream?"

I shook my head no.

"How do you feel about your father now?"

The rocking stopped. "I hate him."

"Why do you hate him?"

"Because he's mean. He's not nice and I always feel uncomfortable around him."

"Uncomfortable in what way?"

"He tells dirty jokes and he's the only one who thinks they're funny." I began to rub my right arm with my left hand. "Half the time I don't even get what he's talking about."

"Why are you rubbing your arm?"

"I can feel him."

"Your dad?"

"Yeah, my dad. He always stood too close to me, especially when he talked to me. Not that we ever had a conversation. I don't think we did. I mean just in general. I remember one time when our whole family attended a wedding together, my father announced to everyone that he wanted all of "his girls" to dance with him. Sherry and Jane danced with him, but I wouldn't. My mom even pleaded with me to do it. She said she didn't want to see my father hurt like that. But I wouldn't do it. Just the thought of it made my skin crawl."

"Why was that?"

"I don't know. It's just always been that way since I was a little girl. When we were small he used think it was great fun to put all three of us into the bathtub at the same time and give us a bubble bath. My sisters never seemed to mind, but I hated it."

"Anne, this is really important. Will you try to remember why you didn't like it?"

"Sure. But I'm starting to get another one of my headaches and I don't know how much longer I can last. Why won't you tell me what you think my dream meant?"

"Let's try and work through the headache this time. Tell me, if you can, what it was about your father bathing you that you didn't like."

"I didn't like my father giving me a bath because . . . Wow, this is hard. Okay, let me start again. I didn't like my father giving me a bath because he scared me. I was afraid he was going to do something to me. Now, off hand, I don't know what that would've been. The last time I can remember him bathing us, I ended up jumping out of the tub covered in suds and running to the doorway. When I got to the doorway, I put my hand on the doorknob and yelled at my sisters. 'Get out! Get out!' "

"What made you do that?"

"I didn't like him bathing me."

"What did your father do?"

"He just laughed his stupid laugh and said, 'What's wrong with you? We're only having fun.'"

"How old were you then?"

"Six. Wow, all of the sudden I'm getting sick to my stomach."

"Are you going to be okay?"

I nodded my head yes.

"Can I ask you where your mother was during at this time?"

"My mother? My mother wasn't there. She worked nights

at the hospital and if she wasn't working, she was trying to sleep."

The therapist let out a big sigh. "Anne, I truly wish I didn't have to be the one to tell you this, but what I think we're talking about here is incest. Everything in your dream and everything you've told me today leads me to believe that's what we're dealing with. I also think that the reason your sisters appeared in the dream with you is that they were incested as well."

From the moment I heard the word incest I felt myself disappear. It was as if the therapist was speaking to a ghost and the real Anne was floating somewhere out in space, shrouded in fog.

"Anne . . . Anne!"

"What?"

"Where are you?"

"Here."

"Well, you scared me."

"I'm sorry." I knew I was having a conversation because I could hear myself talking, but my voice seemed to be coming from another part of my body. I knew I was crying because I could feel the tears roll down my face, but it was as if it was happening to someone else, not me.

"What are thinking about?"

"Nothing."

"Nothing?"

"Well, actually there is something. I was thinking about trust."

"Trust?"

"Yes, I was thinking how awful it must be for someone to be six years old and not be able to trust anybody." Then I reached for the box of tissues sitting at my feet and began to sob.

"Anne."

The therapist pulled his chair slightly in my direction and the movement startled me. "Don't you touch me," I snarled. "Don't you ever touch me!"

"I wasn't going to touch you," he responded calmly. "I was only going to move my chair in a little closer."

"Well, don't! I hate it when people try to comfort me. That moving-of-your-chair business is just another way to try and comfort me. Don't you ever pat my knee, squeeze my hand, put your arm around my shoulder, or move your chair in closer to me if I'm crying. I hate it. All of it. Is that clear?"

"It's clear."

The fog lifted. I was back in my own body. "This thing with my dad. It's only a theory, right?"

"That's right."

"So, there's a chance it may not be true, right?

"It might not . . . but, Anne, you're awfully angry at your dad. You're so angry with him that at the end of this dream you stab him with a butcher knife."

"Yeah, that's true. Well look, if it's okay with you I'd like to quit for today. I need to think about this for awhile."

"That's fine . . . but I need you to promise me something before you walk out of here today."

"What?"

"That you'll call me if you find yourself in too much pain."

I heard my voice say, "I'll call you if I'm in too much pain." But the voice came from such a distant part of my body it didn't sound like me. It was the voice chanting inside my head that sounded familiar. *Liar! You'll never call him and you know it.*

• • •

"The sky is falling! The sky is falling!" said Chicken Little to Henny Penney.

Cracked. Fractured. Splintered.

What's that cracking noise? I wondered as I drove home from my appointment that afternoon. And then all of sudden I knew—it was me. I had started to come apart.

Humpty Dumpty sat on a wall. Humpty Dumpty had a great fall.

There were large cracks in my body. I couldn't see them, of course, but I knew they were there all the same.

Cracked. Fractured. Splintered. I'd fallen off the wall.

"The sky is falling," I cried out in agony and pulled off the road.

I have no memory of the rest of the afternoon. I have no memory of anything at all until the moment I opened my front door and saw the girls on the floor watching *Sesame Street* on the television.

I closed the door and made my way to the sofa.

"Where have you been?" Bob's voice dripped in sarcasm. "When I left this morning, you said you were going to pick up the girls after school today and then go straight to work. The next thing I know, you're calling me at work and telling me you have no way to get them."

So I did call him.

"You don't tell me why. You just say you can't do it. Well, I'm not stupid, Anne. Right after you called me, I called your hospital. And, you know what they told me? They told me you'd called in sick for the day."

So, I must have called them as well. I laid my head on the arm of the sofa and closed my eyes.

"I think you're having an affair. So, why don't you just tell me the truth about what's going on, because quite honestly, Anne, I don't know how you can live with yourself."

"I don't either."

At some point, I became aware that I could stand outside myself and see myself as others saw me. I could see myself putting my head down on the sofa. I could hear myself talking to Bob. Somehow, I had split off from myself and I was no longer alone. It was a comforting feeling. The hole in my chest left by the exploding incest bomb was filling up.

"I don't know what's going on." I kept my eyes closed. "I don't understand it myself. I got this huge migraine after my therapy appointment and knew I couldn't go into work. That's all. Thanks for picking up the girls. If you need to get back to church feel free to go. I'll be okay. "

"That's it? That's all you're going to say? You were supposed to be home two hours ago. What were you doing all that time?"

"Driving around. That's all. Just driving around. When I started to get sick I stopped the car and went to sleep." I didn't know if I was telling the truth or not. I had no idea what had happened to the time.

It was getting close to dinnertime and I knew that if Bob didn't leave I'd have to get up and fix dinner. I had to get him out of there. All I wanted to do was take the girls to McDonald's for a hamburger. Why couldn't he just accept what I was saying and go?

I opened my eyes and looked at him. "If you don't believe me, that's fine. I just don't want to talk anymore. My head is pounding. I'm sorry I upset your schedule today. I know this was a busy day for you. The girls and I can go out for something to eat if you need to get back to church."

Bob didn't know whether to believe me or not.

I waited.

"Well," he finally said. "I guess I'll go back."

As soon as Bob left, Kim dragged her tattered blue flowered comforter across the floor and sat down beside me. Tina climbed onto the sofa and started to cry.

I gathered them close to me. "Hey you guys, everything's going to be fine. When *Sesame Street*'s over I promise I'll get up and take you to McDonalds. Just let me lay here a little bit longer until my headache gets better. Okay?"

As soon as their program ended I kept my promise. But my headache never went away. No matter how many Excedrin I took. It was still there. I took so many Excedrin that by the end of the evening my ears rang and my skin itched. But the headache never went away.

I pulled a chair in front of the television set after I'd put the girls to bed, then turned the volume down and stared at the screen. I had no idea what was on. From time to time I rested my head on the back of the chair and prayed, "God, please let me die."

Bob came home at eleven o'clock and with a sideward glance in my direction, walked down the hallway to his bedroom. "I guess you're feeling better. Goodnight."

I stared at the television set until well after midnight. "Where are you now, God?" I asked as I gently lowered my pounding head onto the pillow and let the coolness of the bed sheets comfort me. "If You even exist and You can hear me, please let me die. I don't want to wake up in the morning. I mean it. I've had it. I cannot take another day."

Chapter Eighteen

You'll Never Be Free

But I didn't die, and with the arrival of a new day came a new discovery. I found out that what oxygen is to a dying patient, so routine is to someone who is losing her mind.

I clung to the needs of my children much like a drowning person clings to a life raft. Their routine gave me stability. Their existence gave me a reason to go on.

The morning after the incest bomb had exploded I showered, dressed and went to wake the girls.

Then just as their little feet reached out to touch the blue braided circular area rug covering the hard wood floor, a scene suddenly exploded in front my eyes. It happened so fast and burned with such intensity that my hand flew up and grabbed my head.

I saw myself as a six-year-old child lying in bed and could hear my father's footsteps ascending the stairs. I saw his shadow as he entered the bedroom and heard him walk by the double bed in which my sisters slept. My eyes were closed but I knew what he was there for.

I grabbed the edge of my blankets and pulled them closer to my face as my father stood over me and whispered, "Get up."

I felt his vice-like grip on my shoulder and started to cry. He repeated his command. "I said get up."

My white flannel nightgown with tiny pink roses on it skimmed the tops of my feet as I reached for the floor.

The desperation of the day before returned. "You guys go brush your teeth," I said forcing myself to remain calm. "I'll get your clothes for school today and then go fix your breakfast."

I went into the kitchen, opened the cupboard doors and stared at the cereal boxes. I couldn't decide what to feed them. My mind was a blank

I opened the refrigerator, but quickly closed the door. The refrigerator light hurt my eyes.

I sat down at the kitchen counter and squeezed my head between my hands. "I'm going crazy. I know I am. Please God, don't let me go crazy. Please. Not here. Not now." I felt frozen by time.

It was Tina who rescued me. "Mommy," she yelled down the hall. "I can't find my tennis shoe. Kimmy already has her's on and she won't help me find mine."

I don't have time to go crazy. Not now. Not today. I have children to raise. I stood up. "I'll be right there!"

As the day progressed I began to tell myself what I was doing as I was doing it. When I left for the grocery store, I said, "Now you're going to the grocery store." When I went to work I said, "Now you're going to work."

Mercifully, while I was at the hospital, the routine of the job took over. By telling myself what I was doing as I was doing it, my grip on reality, though tenuous, became stronger.

The following day, Bob left early in the morning for a choir retreat and didn't return home until late that night.

I was in bed when he knocked on my door. "Annie, are you asleep?"

"No."

He walked in and sat on the edge of my bed. "I need to talk to you."

His quick movements and the fierce look in his eyes scared me. I didn't want him anywhere near me.

I sat up and even though I was wearing a nightgown, grabbed the sheet, pulling it in close to my chin. I spoke in a whisper. "What do you want?"

"Annie," He said as he stroked my leg with his hand. "Annie . . . I've missed you so much."

The pleading voice. The strength in his hands. The look in his eyes. I'd heard it before. I'd seen it before. But not from Bob. From my father. I gripped the sheet tighter. My hands shook.

I couldn't think. I couldn't move.

He slid his hand up my inner thigh.

I pulled my leg away.

"Annie, please don't pull away from me like that. I need you so much." He fondled my breast, caressed my face, neck and shoulders.

I felt paralyzed. Tears streamed down my face. "Leave me alone," I whispered.

"Oh, Annie, I wish I could. But I can't. I still love you so much it hurts." He took my face in his hands. "Let me make love to you just one more time."

I jerked away. "Don't do that."

Once more he cupped his hands around my face. He kissed my face. My hair. My neck. His breathing became harder as he whispered in my ear, "Please, please do this for me."

My father . . . Bob.

Bob . . . my father.

It was all the same.

In confusion and pain I shook my head back and forth. Then like a cat that had been cornered, I sat up, arched my back and leaned in towards his face.

"STOP TOUCHING ME," I hissed. "I HATE IT!"

And in that instant the desire in Bob's eyes dissolved into hatred. "Hate it? You used to love it," he snarled.

Anne, don't say anything.

The air felt so heavy, I could hardly breathe. Nothing moved.

A small voice shattered the stillness. "Mommy!"

Neither one of us spoke.

"Mommy!"

Time hung suspended.

"Bob, I've got to see what she wants."

He got up and made his way to the door. "You're never going to be free of me, never. Because in God's eyes you'll always be mine."

I waited until I heard him go into the bathroom before I got out of bed to check on the girls. "Is Daddy home?" Kim asked, her voice groggy with sleep.

"Yes, sweetheart, he is. Kimmy, do you think you can go back to sleep now? Tomorrow is Sunday and we have church in the morning." She nodded and eased her head back onto her pillow.

As I was making my way back to bed another scene explosion occurred, and just as before it was a scene from my past that seared my brain.

Again I am in bed, but this time it was my mother not my father, who is standing over me. "What on earth ever possessed you to do such a thing?" Her voice was full of anger. "You're six years old. You should know better that this! If you vomit in the middle of the night you need to wake someone up. Now look at this. It's all over everything. Your pillow. Your sheets. Your nightgown. It's even in your hair!"

I could feel my back pressing harder and harder into the wall trying to get away from her.

As with the first, it was over in a matter of seconds. I climbed back into bed. "I want to die," I sobbed over and over again. "I want to die. I want to die. I want to die."

When I awoke the following morning I couldn't remember what day it was. When I finally realized it was Sunday, the day came into focus. Bob should've been up already, and the girls needed to get up and dressed for church. I opened the door to their bedroom and was surprised when I found Kim's bed empty.

She must be watching television. I hurried down the short hallway to the living room. She wasn't there. Nor was she in the kitchen, or the bathroom. That only left one place. I opened the door to Bob's bedroom and found Kim asleep with her father in his king-size bed.

My heart pounded as I shook him awake. "Just what do you think you're doing?"

Kim woke up. "Mommy what's wrong?" I ignored her.

"Did you think that if I wouldn't sleep with you then maybe your six-year-old daughter would do just fine?"

Bob looked sleepy and confused. "You're crazy, you know that? I didn't even know Kimmy was here. She must have crawled into bed with me after I went to sleep."

Kim started to cry. "Mommy, did I do something wrong? Please don't be mad at Daddy."

He reached over and comforted her. "No, Kimmy, of course you didn't do anything wrong. Your mommy is just a very sick person."

I backed up to the doorway and grabbed onto the doorknob for support. "I'm sorry Kim. I'm sorry I got so upset with you and I'm sorry I got so upset with Daddy. And you know what? Everybody needs to start getting ready for church or we're not going to make it on time."

I held out my hand as Kim crawled to the edge of the bed. "And you know what else? I think we'll go to the church where I go to Bible Study instead of Daddy's"

"No," Kim whimpered. "I want to go to Daddy's. I like the people there. They're really nice to me."

I knelt down beside her and stroked her hair. "Kimmy, please don't cry. I don't want to go to Daddy's church today. But I'll make a deal with you. If you go with me to my church today, then next week on Easter, we can go to Daddy's. Remember how much fun Daddy's church is on Easter? We'll get you a new dress and everything."

"Wait a minute," Bob said now fully awake with his feet on the floor. "You mean you're not going to go with me to church today? I thought we'd agreed you would only go to that church of yours for Bible Study."

"Bob, please." I stood up and continued to stroke Kim's hair. "Let's just try and get out the door this morning without a huge fight. I just need some space, that's all. We'll go with you next Sunday, I promise."

Kim remained at my side sucking her thumb.

Bob opened his mouth to say something, but then changed his mind. I held my breath and waited. "Just this once and only because I'm out of time. Otherwise I'd dress the girls myself and bring them with me. I want you to meet me after church in the choir room. Otherwise people are going to talk. I'll make an excuse for you. I'll tell them you're sick."

I'd just bought myself four hours of freedom.

I was going to Bel-Air, but I had no intention of going to the Sunday morning service. I wanted to find Margaret. She'd been there for me when I needed a psychologist. She'd been there for me when I needed an attorney. I hoped and prayed she'd be there for me now.

I dropped the girls off in Sunday school and went looking for her. It didn't take long. I found her on the patio outside the sanctuary talking with a group of women. As I approached the women grew quiet.

"Can I see you for a moment, Margaret?"

Margaret turned to the group and smiled. "Will you excuse me?"

A few feet from the group I whispered rather loudly, "I can't wait until June. I'm leaving Bob today."

"Anne, dear, I think we need to talk about this privately. Let's discuss this in my office."

Margaret closed the door to her small office overlooking the Santa Monica Mountains. Two upholstered chairs filled up the corner. Margaret sat in one. I sat in the other, crying.

"Anne, tell me what's happened that's made you want to leave today."

"Because, I can't stand living with him anymore. That's why. When church is over I'm going to go home, pack my suitcases and leave. I don't know where I'll go, but it doesn't make any difference. You know I'll be able to find work anywhere I go, so where I end up isn't all that important. I just cannot take one more minute with him. He drives me crazy.

He quotes Scripture to me and I shake. He tells me he has God and the whole church on his side and I cry. Not just some of the time. All of the time. I hate him. I cannot take one more minute of this."

"Where are the children now?"

"They're here. Please don't try and talk me out of this, Margaret. He really is driving me crazy and I just wanted somebody to know what I'm doing."

"Do you have any money saved?"

I got up and started to pace. "No."

"Do you have enough money in your checking account?"

"I have some money. But I can get a job right away and ask them to pay me as soon as I finish the shift. I can do this, Margaret. I know I can. I just can't go back to that house!"

"I thought you had agreed with your attorney to file in June. Did something specific happen to bring on this crisis?"

"What difference does it make what happened? I want out! Now!"

"Anne, stop pacing. Please sit down and tell me what happened."

"He pressured me for sex last night." I sobbed and collapsed into the chair.

"What did you do?"

"I told him to leave me alone."

"And did he?"

"Yes. But that doesn't change anything."

"Is that all?"

"What do you mean, 'Is that all?' Isn't that enough?"

"Well, of course it is, dear. I'm just trying to understand everything."

"You can't make me go back there." I folded my arms over my chest.

"You cannot take the children and leave, Anne. If you do, he'll call it kidnapping and file charges. He'll also claim that since you were the one that left, you abandoned the house. Once that happens you'll have given Bob everything he needs to file for full custody and ultimately you'll be the one who had to move out."

"You don't know what you're asking me to do," I wailed. "You've never even been divorced!"

"Anne, I am divorced. How do you think I was able to refer you to an attorney so quickly?"

So great was my distress that her news hardly registered with me.

"You can't make me go back, you know."

"No, of course I can't."

I drummed my fingers against the armrest of the chair and wiped away the tears.

"If I go back and he pressures me for sex again, I won't be able to stand it. I know I won't."

"I don't think he will, but if he does, simply tell him no."

"Well, if I do go back, and I'm not saying I will, but if I do I'm going to get all my records together and bring them to the attorney first thing tomorrow morning. I want him to file for my divorce no later than June."

"I think that's exactly what you should do. Will you call me after you've seen the attorney?"

"Maybe. Maybe not."

"Well, will you call your therapist and tell him what we talked about today?"

"I'm not calling him. He only makes things worse."

"Anne, the only thing your therapist and I want to do is help. I know you're angry with me right now, but all I want is what best for you and the girls."

I ignored Margaret's last remark and looked at my watch. "I guess it's time for church to be over." I got up from the chair, threw my purse over my shoulder and headed for the door. "I'd better go get Kim and Tina from Sunday school."

"Before you leave I think we need to pray about this."

"I don't want to pray."

"Well, will you let me give you a hug?"

I waved her off. "I'm in too much pain right now. I'm going to do as you asked, Margaret, but I can't guarantee how long I'll last."

"I understand. But, please call me before you do anything drastic."

It was useless to go on. Margaret was never going to understand how desperate I was. Her answer to everything was "Let's pray about this."

I left defeated and determined. The divorce attorney was getting a call from me first thing Monday morning.

I never talked privately to Margaret again. With every passing day she was sounding more and more like Bob to me.

The phone call to the attorney's office on Monday galvanized me. I wasn't going to let anything stop me from getting my freedom. Not bad memories from my childhood, not the church, not Bob, not even my fear of the unknown. I wanted to be free—with or without Biblical grounds for a divorce. June first was set as the official date for my divorce papers to be filed.

Thursday arrived and with it my usual therapy appointment.

"How are you doing, Anne?"

Something in the way he asked the question made me wary. I instantly went on alert.

"Why did you say it like that?"

"Like what?"

"I don't know like what. There's something in your voice that makes me uncomfortable."

"I'm sorry. I didn't mean to make you uncomfortable. So, how are you?"

"I'm okay. Look, are you annoyed with me for some reason?"

He hesitated. "Margaret called me today."

"Margaret called you today? About me?"

"Yes. She was concerned. "

"Well, now that's just great. And just what did the two of you talk about because she was so concerned?"

"She wanted me to aware of the fact that you'd had a rough weekend."

"Did she also happen to mention somewhere in all of her concern that I wanted to leave and she told me not to do it?"

"Yes."

"Boy, I'll just bet the two of you had a great time talking about everything. She probably didn't stop there, either. She probably went on to tell you that Bob pressured me for sex and maybe that's where you might have mentioned your theory about what my dad had been up to when I was six?"

"Obviously, we didn't talk about anything that was confidential."

"Oh, who knows what the two of you really talked about!"

"Can I ask you why you are so upset about Margaret's phone call?"

"Yes, you can! It feels like the two of you have been talking behind my back. If I'd wanted you to know what had happened to me over the weekend, I would have told you myself. I don't need Margaret talking things over with you or anybody. My mother used to do that to me all the time. It didn't make any difference what was going on. If it was about me, the whole neighborhood knew. Nothing was ever left private. Once she even told an entire room full of relatives when I got my period. So if it's all the same to you, I don't want you talking to Margaret about me . . . or anybody else for that matter. You'll know if I think I can't handle something. You got it?"

"That's fine with me, but can I ask one more question?"

"Go ahead."

"Why do you think you have to handle everything on your own?"

"That is such a stupid question I can't believe you asked it! Because I am alone! Or haven't you noticed? My mother has told me not to call if I get divorced. My father's been gone so long from the picture I can't even remember what he looks like. All but one of my church friends has gone into hiding. Bob says he has his whole church on his side. And Margaret . . . Well, Margaret sounds more and more like Bob every day. So from where I sit, I think that's pretty much it."

"But people like Margaret and me are here to help you."

"That's great. But you know something? I don't want to talk about Margaret anymore. I'm sick of talking about Margaret. I want to talk about last week's session."

"What about last week's session?"

"I decided I probably made the whole thing up about my dad. Well, maybe not the whole thing because he actually did bathe us, but I certainly don't think it was as bad as you seem to think it was. I could have gotten out of the tub because the water was too hot . . . or too cold, even. Or maybe the soap was stinging my eyes. There, that's it. The soap must have been stinging my eyes."

"You mean, you don't think your father molested you."

"No, I don't. And, I wish you wouldn't use that word. I hate it. I know he wasn't the nicest man in the whole world and he did have a terrible temper, but I seriously doubt that someone who was a Colonel in the Army and a decorated war hero would ever do something like that. It hardly seems that given the code of conduct they have to live by—you know that duty, honor, country thing—that he'd ever do anything like that. I don't know why I had those dreams, but that's all they were, just dreams."

"Anne, I think your dreams tell us something more than you're willing to accept about your father. It's not my job to force you to believe anything, but it is my opinion he did molest you. So let me caution you that as time goes on you might experience scenes from your childhood that may flash before your eyes and then disappear. You probably won't have any warning before they come and before you can really concentrate on them, they'll be gone. If they come, don't fight them. Just let them come. I could be wrong. You may not have them at all. I'm only trying to prepare you in case they do. I also think you think I shouldn't have accepted Margaret's phone call. Am I right?"

"About what?" I was exhausted and once again my voice seemed very far away.

"Do you feel I shouldn't have accepted Margaret's phone call?"

"I don't know what you should have done. I'm sort of confused right now. But yeah, I guess you shouldn't have accepted it. You could have said hello and stuff, just not talked about me."

"Well, I hope by the time you leave today you'll feel that your trust is something I've worked very hard to earn and I wouldn't intentionally do anything to jeopardize it."

Why couldn't I get the therapist to agree with me?

My emotional strength depended on my being able to convince myself that my dreams had been meaningless. There had to be a perfectly logical explanation to my father's behavior. There just had to be.

"You know it's a waste of time to go on talking about my dad. In six weeks I'm going to file for divorce and I need to focus on that. I need a plan for myself and the girls because I have no idea how Bob will react when they serve him with divorce papers."

"You're really not going to deal with this, are you Anne?"

"Deal with what?"

The therapist shook his head. "Fine. Let's talk about how you're going to prepare yourself for what happens when they file your papers."

• • •

My attorney called. "Do you think Bob would be willing to come in and pick up the divorce papers so we can avoid the process server?"

"What's a process server?"

"Someone you pay to deliver the papers into his hands. We can avoid the cost if he would come in and pick them up."

"He's not going to do that. Couldn't we just mail them?"

"No," the attorney said. I could hear a smile in his voice. "The law requires us to make certain he gets them in person. So why don't you make a copy of Bob's schedule and mail it to me."

"Sure, okay." I sounded confident but it wasn't clear to me that any of this was going to work at all.

Kim's first grade teacher called. Kim had been coming to school in tears. The teacher was concerned and requested a conference. Tina's preschool teacher called. Tina's normally sweet disposition had disappeared. Could I come in for a conference? I met with both of their teachers.

Kim's allergies were growing progressively worse.

"Stop asking me to find another medication," the allergist said after our second visit to his office in a week.

"The only thing that will help your daughter is for you to fix her destructive home life." I was stunned by his reprimand. I'd never had anyone speak to me so boldly before. How did he know about my marriage? Had Kim said something? I was too embarrassed to ask. I simply added it on to my growing list as one more reason to get out of the marriage.

I needed a plan. I needed a plan to be anywhere but in Los Angeles when the papers were served. And this time I wasn't going to tell Margaret anything.

Chapter Nineteen

Strength Beyond Endurance

I called my friend Linda in the first week of May. Linda and I had worked together in the Intensive Care Unit at St. Joseph's in Burbank, and we had shared a common bond: our children were exactly the same age. Our friendship grew steadily until Linda's husband was transferred to San Francisco, but we'd managed to stay in touch through letters and had frequently made promises to visit one another. If anyone would be willing to help, I was sure it would be Linda. Still, my hand trembled when I picked up the phone.

"Hi Linda. It's me, Anne."

"Anne," she exclaimed. "What a wonderful surprise. How is everything? Or is that why you're calling me?" I found Linda's warm and reassuring voice instantly comforting.

"Actually, that is sort of why I'm calling. I was wondering if it would be possible for me to bring the girls up for a visit the first week of June?"

"Absolutely! The boys are going to love it, and now that I'm only working part-time at a doctor's office we'll be able to have lots of time to catch up on everything. How long can you stay?"

"Probably for a couple of days. I think I'll drive over and take a look at Lake Tahoe as well."

"That sounds perfect. I'll get the guestroom ready. You're driving up here, right?"

"Yes, and do you think you can mail me directions? I don't want to take all that information down over the phone. I've been so confused lately, I'd probably get it all wrong."

"No problem. How's it going with Bob?"

"I'll tell you all about it when I get there."

"It's bad?"

"It's bad. Thanks for letting us come, Linda."

"Don't be silly. I can hardly wait to tell the boys. They'll be so excited! So look, you send me arrival plans and I'll send you directions."

I fought back tears of relief as I hung up the phone. The first part of my plan was complete. Now all I had to do was tell Bob. I waited until the last week in May. Time was running out.

"Bob, I need to talk to you," I said as I walked in the door from my shift at the hospital.

Bob sat in front of the television absorbed in the *Tonight Show* and barely acknowledged my presence.

I sat down on the sofa. "I need you to know I'm going ahead with the divorce. The papers are going to be filed on June first."

He refused to look at me. "And just where do you think you're going to get the money to pay for an attorney?"

"It doesn't matter. The only thing you need to know is that I'm going to do it. The attorney wants to know if you'd be willing to come in and pick up the papers."

"No."

"Fine, then. They'll have to be served. One other thing—the girls and I are planning to visit Linda and David in San Francisco. We're leaving the day the papers are filed and we'll return a week later."

"You're driving," he asked with a sideward glance in my direction.

"Yes."

"I'll be here when you get back," he said staring at the television.

My legs almost gave way when I got up from the sofa. I had to force myself to place one foot in front of the other as I walked out of the room. But I had done it. I had told him.

On the morning of June first, I called the attorney and when he assured me everything was on schedule, I hung up the phone and loaded up the car.

The girls were excited and very determined to help in packing. Their main concern was, "Can we stay in a motel with a swimming pool?" Once they had their swimsuits packed, they were stumped as to what else to bring. Bob pulled up just as we were putting the cooler filled with drinks and snacks into the backseat.

His surprise visit annoyed me. "What are you doing here? I thought you were supposed to be working."

"I am. But I wanted to give my girls a proper good-bye." To their squeals and giggles, he picked them up and swung them around in the air.

Then quite unexpectedly, he leaned over and tried to kiss me.

I jerked my head away. "Have you gone completely mad?" I hissed and climbed into the car.

Bob waved and shouted to us as we drove off. "Have a wonderful time! I'll miss you!"

We headed north up Interstate 5 and with each passing mile I felt my confidence level surge upward. "I can't believe I'm actually doing this," became my mantra. By the time we hit our first bathroom stop at a gas station near Bakersfield I was ecstatic. Kim and Tina immediately leaped out of the car and ran to the Coke machine. "We can do this," I yelled to the sky as I followed behind them. "I know we can do this."

Kim and Tina turned out to be seasoned travelers. Their cross-country trips to North Dakota made the eight-hour trip to San Francisco seem quite ordinary by comparison. No sooner had we arrived at Linda and David's than the girls were off playing with their friends in the backyard.

I screamed with delight when Linda came walking down the sidewalk. "You didn't tell me you were pregnant!"

Linda smiled and hugged me. "I figured you'd find our soon enough. Besides, I wanted to wait until we found out the results of the sonogram yesterday."

"And?"

"It's a girl!"

"Fabulous!" We walked arm and arm towards the house. "I know you guys have wanted a little girl for a long time now."

"I'll get David to check on the children and then I want you to fill me in on everything before we start dinner."

Linda's family room had a great view of the back yard. I sank into the sofa. "Your house is huge! It's quite a change from your two bedroom apartment."

"This place is so big that, as you can see, we don't even have enough furniture to fill it. I'm going to take a minute to get us some iced tea. But I want you to keep talking. Tell me what's been going on."

Just then David entered the room. "Hey, Linda, let me get the ice tea. Then maybe you girls will let me join you." David threw me a conspiratorial wink.

When we were settled, I looked over at David with his enormous dark eyes and gentle nature as he sat on the ottoman next to Linda. Not only did they look alike—they were partners in every way. Where Linda was excitable, David was calm. He helped her with the boys. She helped him in his business. It was hard not to be envious.

"I just saw Kim in the backyard," David said "and she looks wonderful. You did a fantastic job with her, Anne. I thought from the sounds of things there would have been a lot more scarring. She really looks great."

"She still has scars on her leg, but that's about it."

"Well, you're to be commended. It couldn't have been easy." When David pushed his ottoman closer to Linda's chair, something in that simple gesture touched me deeply. I felt my throat tighten.

"So," David continued, "tell us. What's been going on?"

"Well, I guess the most important thing is that I filed the papers this morning. I don't mean that I filed them, personally. The attorney filed them. Bob should get them in a couple of days."

The minute the words were out of my mouth the enormity of what I'd done hit me. Only the sounds of the playing children filtering through the glass patio doors helped me maintain my composure.

Linda was genuinely moved. "Anne, I am so sorry. Do you want to tell us about it? I don't want to pressure you, but we sure would love to support you in anyway we could."

"It's no pressure. I want somebody to know what it's been like, but I'm afraid I'll make a spectacle of myself. I cry all the time now. It's really embarrassing."

"Oh, please, Anne. I cry all the time. And believe it or not, even boys have been known to do it."

"Well," I said as I reached for the tissue, "I guess I'll start with the end first. Bob thinks I blame him for the fire and I don't. I have a lot of resentment about the fire, but Bob never caused it and I know that. What I blame him for is what he did afterwards."

"What did he do?"

"He did nothing!" I slammed my fist into my knee. "He sees Kim on fire and he does nothing!"

"Anne, I certainly don't mean to defend Bob, but he did try to put the fire out with his hands. I think that's at least something."

"Okay, fine, that's something. But everybody knows you can't put a fire out with your hands! At least not one as big as that one was. See," I said pointing to my face. "It's no use. I am going to make a spectacle of myself."

"We have boxes of tissues in every room of this house," David said as he handed one from the nearby coffee table. "It's no problem."

"Thanks. Anyway, when we got home, I wanted Bob to write the company he'd worked for in North Dakota and ask them to pay Kim's hospital expenses. But he didn't want to do it. He said that it wasn't the company's fault that Kim got cold and climbed out of bed. But then he said, 'and, besides, if I ask them to pay, they may not hire me back next year.'"

David looked stunned. "Wait a minute. Are you telling me that Kim comes within seconds of burning to death and

Bob didn't want to do anything because he's afraid he's going to lose his summer job?"

I nodded my head. "So I wrote them. I probably wouldn't have done it at all except I didn't think we should have to pay for Kim's hospital bills. I felt they owed us that much. I wanted Bob to stand up for us. I wanted him to say his family was more important than his career. But he couldn't do it."

"Anne, I don't think anyone can understand what you must have gone through," Linda said sympathetically. "But isn't there any hope for the marriage at all? I thought once Bob got the job in the church things would've gotten better."

"The job at the church came too late."

"Have you thought about marriage counseling?" David asked. "I'm sure Linda must have told you that we saw a counselor soon after we found out we were going to be transferred. It was Linda's idea, but I thought it was a pretty good one. You know, sometimes all you need is someone else's perspective on things."

"David, Bob won't go to a counselor. He thinks they're Satanic."

"Satanic?" Linda and David said together.

Their surprise made me smile. "Yes. He thinks counselors are Satanic. Lots of people in the fundamental church think like that. Ministers as counselors are fine, but if you go to anybody else, you're opening yourself to the possibility that Satan will get hold of your mind."

"Well, you don't believe that. Do you?" Linda looked skeptical.

"No, but an awful lot of people do. Actually, I've been getting help from a therapist ever since the fire."

"Oh, that's good," Linda sighed and threw David a glance.

David leaned forward, put his elbows on his knees and gently patted his fingertips together. "Sounds to me like you don't have much choice."

I nodded my head. "I hope you guys don't think I came to this decision one night out of frustration or just because of the fire. It's been difficult for a long, long time and lately it's been impossible. I just can't live with him any longer. I feel like I'm dying."

"This whole thing makes me so sad," Linda said with tears in her eyes. "I feel bad for everybody. You . . . the girls . . . Bob."

"Bob?"

"Anne, you know Bob loves you. He may be messed up, but you know he loves you. Besides, the girls are crazy about him. They're going to take this really hard."

Linda's response stunned me. I'd anticipated she'd say something supportive of me, not Bob. I didn't want to hear from anybody how hard it was going to be on the girls, or that Bob still loved me. I already knew that and hearing it from Linda only reinforced my sense of overwhelming guilt. "Look, Linda," I snapped. "Whose side are you on anyway? I know Bob loves me and the girls are going to take this really hard, but I can't live with him any longer. Besides, according to him I just really never got 'It.' Whatever the magic fundamental Baptist 'It' was. I wasn't submissive enough. I definitely wasn't supportive enough. But if you want to know the truth, the real problem was I couldn't make him famous. Fame is like a drug to him.

It's all he ever thinks about. He needs an audience to feel alive not a family. If you want to feel bad for Bob, feel bad because he isn't famous. Not because I'm going to divorce him."

"I don't think Linda meant to take sides," David said reaching out for Linda's hand. "I think she only meant to say that this is a really sad thing for all of you."

I sat on the sofa unable to look at anything but the floor. "I'm sorry I went nuts. My nerves are completely shot."

Suddenly, the kitchen door flew open and all four of the children burst into the family room.

Roger, the oldest of Linda's two boys and the one most like her, spoke out instantly. "Hey! Why is everybody crying?"

"It was only a misunderstanding," David said as he got up from the ottoman. Then he clapped his hands together and with a big grin on his face he said, "I'll bet the reason all of you came charging in here is because you're all hungry. Am I right?"

"Right," yelled the boys.

Kim and Tina said nothing. They stared at me with eyes filled with concern and apprehension.

The time with David and Linda flew by.

"So, what's going to happen once you get back to L.A.?" Linda asked as she walked me out to the car.

"I don't know really. The papers should have been served by now and I'm hoping he'll be gone by the time I get back."

"How are you for money?"

"I think I'm going to be alright. I'm starting a new job at UCLA next month and they pay quite a bit more than I make right now."

"Well, let us know if you need anything."

Good-byes were said as the girls reluctantly got into the car and after spending two days in Lake Tahoe, we headed home.

When Los Angeles was still an hour away, I finally told the girls about the divorce.

Tina looked confused, but Kim was furious.

"No," she screamed. "You are not getting a divorce. Daddy loves us too much."

"Kim, Daddy doesn't want the divorce. I do. This has nothing to do with how much he loves you guys."

"Well, why don't you love him anymore?" she sobbed.

"Oh, honey, this is so complicated."

"What's a divorce?" asked Tina who still spoke with a profound lisp.

"A divorce means Daddy won't be living with us anymore," Kim shouted at her.

"Not ever?"

"No, not ever, because Mom's making him leave. She doesn't love him anymore." Kim's anger continued unabated. "Where's he going to live?"

"I don't know. Probably with your Aunt June or maybe get a place of his own. I'm not sure. We haven't really talked about it."

"You think he's to blame for the fire. Don't you?"

"No, I don't. Why would you say that?"

"Because Daddy told me."

"Well, it's not true."

"I don't want to live with you. If you make Daddy leave, I'm going to go live with him."

"You're not going to go live with your father!"

"Oh yes I am. Daddy loves me more than you do."

"Kim. Tina. Listen to me. We both love you. I'm sorry if you think he loves you more than I do, because it's not true. I'm sorry for absolutely everything, but you are never going to go live with your father. You'll still see him a lot. He just won't be living at the house anymore."

"I hate you," Kim screamed. Then she turned her head

away, stuck her thumb in her mouth and stared out the window.

There was nothing I could do except drive.

Kim saw him before I'd even pulled up to the curb. "Daddy's home!"

"Yeah," Bob shouted from the doorway. "My family's back!"

The girls jumped out as soon as I'd turned off the ignition.

"Mom was wrong! Mom was wrong," Kim chanted all the way up to the house with Tina right behind her.

I stayed in the car unable to move. Nothing made any sense. Why was he still here? What had gone wrong? For several minutes I sat very still and waited for the mythical white knight to come and rescue me.

But no one came.

When I finally got a chance to confront him, Bob was a study in controlled calm. "What are you taking about? I don't know anything about any divorce papers."

"You know very well what I'm talking about. You were supposed to have gotten the divorce papers. Now, where are they?"

He feigned innocence. "Honestly, I have no idea what you're talking about. Nobody gave me anything."

"Well, where were you?"

"What do you mean where was I?"

"Were you here at the house or did you go stay with your sister so they couldn't find you?"

"Annie, I swear to you I was here. It sounds to me like you've put your trust in a pretty lousy attorney. Maybe you should take this as a sign."

"What do you mean, a sign?"

"A sign from God that you're not supposed to go through with this." His calm only intensified my anger.

"You're crazy! You know that? You're absolutely nuts! This is not a sign!"

"The girls are very upset. Kim told me what you said to them on the way home today."

"Of course they're upset. But I'm going to get this divorce no matter how many tricks you try and pull." I stared at him for several seconds and tried to determine if he was telling the truth or not.

My heart was racing. My world was spinning. My mind was mess. I didn't know what to do next. I didn't know who to call or how to get help. "I need to shower," I finally said. "It's been a long trip. I'll fix supper when I get out. Why don't you go play with the girls."

I walked down the hall, closed the door to the bathroom and peeled off my dirty clothes. Dropping them in a pile on the floor, I turned on the water and stepped into the shower. *What did I have to do to get myself out of this marriage?* Overcome with grief and despair, I let the water wash over my tired body. "Dear Jesus, I can't seem to do anything right. You've got to help me. Please. Please. Please help me. I don't know what to do." Suddenly the gleam of my double-edged razor in the soap dish caught my eye. I picked it up and turned it around. "Oh, perfect," I whispered out loud. "This just might do it."

Nothing in my life was going to change. I knew that now. No doctor or attorney in the world was ever going to make any difference. Kim hated me. All of my friends from church had disappeared.

Besides, how many times had my mother told me, "Nobody ever really cared about you. You know that. Don't you? The night you were born there was a war on and that's all anybody talked about. Why, I couldn't even get anyone to take me to the hospital when I went into labor. I had to call a cab. Nope, nobody ever gave two hoots about you and that's the truth."

I laid the razor on my wrist and wondered how much pressure it would take to cut through my skin.

I would have to twist the handle and take the razor blade out of course, but after that it would be easy. I wanted my skin to open up. I wanted to see my blood flow through my fingers down into the water below.

The knock at the door startled me.

"Mama! I'm hungry. When are you coming out?" It was Tina.

I looked down and for the first time saw the razor on my wrist.

"Mommy?"

I put the razor away. "Coming!" I turned off the water and stepped out of the tub. As grabbed a towel and started to dry myself off, I could feel occasional tingling sensations. My body was trying to return to the living. I'd walked out onto the edge and decided not to jump. "Not tonight, Bob," I said toweling myself off faster and faster. "You are not going to get me tonight. Tomorrow, I'm going to call my attorney and straighten this whole thing out. There's an answer. I don't know what it is. But there's an answer."

"Mama! I want to come in!" Tina could be persistent.

I opened the door. "Ah, Tina Leigh," I said with a smile as I bent down and scooped her up. "I can tell you are hungry and dirty, and I can fix them both."

I called my attorney the next morning. "This is Anne,"

was all I managed to get out. I didn't trust my voice to go any further.

"Anne, when did you get home?"

"Yesterday afternoon. He's still here." My voice cracked.

"I wish you'd contacted me before you returned so I could have prepared you. We weren't able to get the papers served. He completely eluded us."

"How could that be? I gave you his schedule." Every word was a struggle. Every breath had become painful.

"I know you did and the server went to his house twice; once at five-thirty in the morning and then again at seven in the evening. He even went to the church but Bob denied who he was. I had no idea it was going to be this difficult, but we'll get these papers served. Trust me on this one."

The next call was to my therapist. This time the words flew out of my mouth.

"He's still here! I don't think I'm ever going to get rid of him."

"Anne, can you take a deep breath and slowly tell me what's going on?"

"Oh, who knows what's going on," I snapped. "All I know is that when I got home yesterday, Bob was waiting at the door acting like nothing was wrong. He said he had no idea what I was talking about when I asked him about the divorce papers."

"Did you call the attorney?"

"Of course, I called the attorney!"

"And what did he say?"

"He said they weren't able to get the papers served. Either Bob wasn't where he should have been or he denied who he was. But you know something? I don't care what the reason was. I'm sick of this whole thing. I'm sick of trying to hang in there. I'm sick of trying to cope. I'm sick of crying all the time. I just want him gone."

"Anne, I hate to do this to you because I know you're not going to like it."

"I know what you're already going to say," I said in a singsong voice. "And, yes, I promise not to harm myself in any way and if I even think bad thoughts, I'll be sure to call you."

"I'm very serious about this. I keep thinking back to the first few weeks in therapy when you became so desperate and didn't tell anyone."

"Yeah, well I'm great now. Can't you tell?"

There was only silence on the line.

"What's the matter? Don't you believe me?"

"I'm not sure that I do."

"I don't think you have much choice."

"Are you going to make it to our regular appointment on Thursday?"

"Yep, I'll be there. You know me. If it's Thursday it must be therapy."

I don't remember anything that happened during the week until Sunday night, and what happened Sunday night I'll never forget.

A week had passed since we'd returned from our trip to San Francisco and Bob had been at church the entire day.

Between services, meetings and rehearsals, it wasn't unusual for him to be gone on Sundays from early morning to late at night. The girls and I were usually in bed by the time he returned and this Sunday was no exception. I was asleep when Bob opened the door to my bedroom and hissed at me. "Get up!"

My stomach clamped down so hard inside my body that it felt like I'd been stabbed. I hesitated.

Bob repeated his command and enunciated every word. "I said. Get. Up!"

I got up and put on my robe.

"Go into the living room."

I shut the door to the girls' bedroom before making my way down the hallway.

Once we were in the living room Bob turned loose his full fury.

"Do you know what's on these papers?" His neck and face muscles bulged with rage. His eyes were filled with hate and contempt. "Do you?"

"I think so," I said in hushed tones.

"You think so?" He continued to speak slowly and deliberately. "You know very well what these are. These, my dear Anne . . . It is Anne, isn't it? That is what you prefer to be called isn't it?"

My tongue felt thick. I couldn't get it to make move. I couldn't make a sound.

"Isn't it?"

Still I was silent.

"Answer me!"

Finally, something came out. "Yes."

"Good. Now we're getting somewhere. I just needed to know who I was dealing with tonight. Because you see, Anne, you are a person I no longer know or recognize. In fact, I have no idea who you really are. Someone named Anne—and I presume that is you—had these papers delivered to me at the end of the church service tonight. Not in my office! Not outside the church after the service! They were delivered during an altar call! Just as people were coming down the aisle to accept Jesus Christ into their lives, this man of Satan walked up to me and handed me these papers."

Bob jabbed his finger into my chest to emphasize each point he was making. I kept backing up until I heard a thump. I'd hit the wall. And still he kept jabbing.

His news stunned me. I didn't realize this was what the attorney had meant when he promised to get the papers served.

"Are you going to just stand there? Have you nothing to say about this unspeakable act you have done to me?"

"I didn't do it."

"No, of course, I know you didn't do it. You had your attorney do it. Apparently, getting this divorce means so much to you that you will do anything—including public humiliation."

Terrified and confused, I looked away.

"Look at me, Anne! I want you to see something."

He rustled through the papers. "Bob, listen to me," I pleaded. "I didn't know they were going to serve you papers during the service. I'd never have let them do it. Never . . . "

He wasn't listening. "Ha! I found it," he said waving the paper in front of my face. "Do you see it?"

"I can see it. But I can't read it."

"Well, let me tell you what it says. It says you are requesting alimony. Alimony! I would rather see you rot in hell. ROT IN HELL before I pay you one dime of alimony. I will not—will not—pay you ten cents. You are the one that wants a divorce. Not me. Do you understand me?"

I nodded my head. "I want to ask you a question." My voice wasn't very strong but at least it was there. "What would Pastor Welling and the congregation think if they could see you now?"

The slightest shift occurred in his facial features. They relaxed—slightly.

"I didn't ask you for alimony. Why would I ask you for alimony? I know you don't have any money."

"Oh, don't lie to me. It's right here in the papers."

"The lawyer said it was just a formality. I have no intention of collecting alimony and I had no idea they would serve you the papers at the altar call. I'm truly sorry."

"Well, you can't get me to leave this house," he said as his eyes filled with tears. "You can have your divorce, but I'm not moving out of this house. And you can't take my children away from me."

I phoned the attorney the next morning.

"Did you know they were going to serve Bob with the papers during the church service?"

"He got served during the service?"

"Yes. He came home and went nuts." My voice faltered. "He really scared me."

"I'm sorry, Anne. All I can say is he made it extremely difficult for them."

"He didn't leave," I whispered.

"I'm sorry. What did you say? I couldn't hear you."

"I said he didn't leave."

"You mean he's still there?" The attorney was incredulous. "Okay, I guess this husband of yours is going to make everything just as hard as he can."

"What if he never leaves?"

"Oh, he'll leave, Anne. He'll leave. Now you're going to have to decide if you want the sheriff to come and escort him out or not."

"I don't. Let me wait awhile to see if he leaves on his own."

And so I waited.

I kept my therapy appointments and waited.

I brought the children to school and to church and waited.

I went to work and waited.

I went grocery shopping and waited.

Six weeks later my waiting came to an abrupt end when I walked in the house just as he was taking his favorite painting off the wall.

I asked the obvious. “You’re leaving?”

“Yes. I just saw an attorney. He told me to leave because he thought you probably couldn’t stand the sight of me. Those are hard words to hear.”

“Where are you going?”

“To my sister’s. I’ll figure things out from there.”

And then he was gone.

I was relieved and happy. I was nervous and terrified. I was grief-stricken and sad. But most of all I was alone.

Chapter Twenty

Alone

I hired full time help for the girls and started a new job at the UCLA Medical Center. With the exception of every other weekend when he came to pick up Kim and Tina, Bob and I barely spoke.

The first final notice from the utility company arrived three weeks after he'd left. It stated we were two months behind on our bill and I had forty-eight hours to get it paid. The following morning our phone service was cut off. That afternoon the mail delivered a notice from the bank. We were sixty days behind on our house note. I drove to the nearest pay phone at the gas station down the street, dropped in my dime, and started yelling the minute Bob answered the phone.

"Why haven't you paid the bills?"

"Annie, what are you taking about?" he asked in his I've-got-you-now irritating calm. It drove my anger higher.

"Stop it, Bob. Just stop it! You know very well what I'm talking about. We're behind in our house payments. The phone service was shut off today and they're going to shut off the water and power."

"I don't see how any of this is my problem. You're the one living there, not me."

"Well, are you at least going to make the house payment?"

"Why should I make payments on a house I don't even live in?"

"Because your children live there. That's why!"

"Anne, Anne, Anne. If the girls need something I'll be more than happy to buy it for them. But I'm not going to give you one red cent."

"You don't get it do you? All my money goes for therapy, babysitters and Tina's pre-school. There's no money left to make house payments that are two months late."

"That, my dear Anne, is your problem. You should have thought before you filed for divorce. And Anne?"

"What!"

"If I find you can't support the girls, I'm going to file for full custody."

"I cannot tell you how much I hate you!" I slammed the receiver down and prayed that God would instantly make me a millionaire. I wanted to look down and find hundred dollar bills scattered on the bottom of the phone booth. I ran my hands through my hair in despair. I had absolutely no idea where I was going to get the money.

And that's when I remembered Linda's offer. "If there's anything you need—just give us a call."

I picked up the phone, dropped in another dime and dialed.

"Hey, Linda, this is Anne." I tried to keep my voice upbeat and cheerful.

"Anne, what's is it? You sound awful."

"I don't have enough money for my bills." The words rushed out. "I thought I was going to, but I just found out Bob's not going to pay the mortgage and the utility bills are overdue. They cut off the phone and Bob's threatened to sue for custody if I can't take care of the girls and . . . "

"How much do you need?"

"Too much."

"Just tell me what you need and we'll get it to you."

"I don't know how much I need. I can't even think right now. Just give me a minute. I need . . . I need . . . "

"Anne, I know this is hard for you. But I don't want to guess how much to send. What if I don't send you enough?"

"Two thousand dollars. I need two thousand dollars. I know it's a lot, but I'll pay you back. You know I will."

"It will be in the mail this afternoon."

"Linda, thank you so much. I'm a good risk, honest I am."

"You're going to make it through this, Anne. I know you will."

I stepped out of the phone booth and heaved a giant of relief. It wasn't a million dollars, but it would get us through.

When Bob realized I'd somehow managed to pay the bills, he was furious.

He started phoning . . . two . . . three. . . four . . . five times a day. "I want my girls and I'm going to get them!"

It was difficult for me to believe the attorney when he said, "Bob's never going to get the girls. Never." But I had to. Any other alternative left me swimming in the sea of despair.

There were problems. Kim was angry and argumentative. She fought with me on almost everything. I took her to see the therapist.

Tina was grief stricken. She started off every day in tears. I took her to the therapist as well. The girls fought with each other constantly. I took them both to the therapist. I was obsessed with getting healthy while at the same time daily survival threatened to consume me.

I was always short of cash. I'd told Bob the truth when I said, "all my money goes for therapy, babysitters and preschool." But life, as difficult as it was, was getting better. There were no more flashbacks. I had neither the time nor the energy for them. When the therapist asked, "Are you ever going to work on your issues with incest?" my answer was always the same: "Maybe later, right now I don't have time. I have too much to do." The day to day struggle to survive had forced my nightmares to become a thing of the past.

And life went on.

I hired a live-in housekeeper and went back to working nights because they paid more money. With the exception of one weekend a month, I was now working all the time.

Gone were the Tuesday morning Bible Studies, Margaret, and all of the friends I'd made before I filed for divorce.

Gone were the people I'd met through Bob's church. Gone was any contact with my family. And Pastor Welling turned out to be right. I was exhausted and completely alone.

Nine months later I sat in the Los Angeles County Courthouse in Van Nuys, California trying to understand the judge's question.

"Do you think this is fair?"

Confused, I looked at my attorney who nodded in the direction of the judge.

"I'm sorry, Your Honor, do I think what is fair?"

"The settlement. You're going to get the house, but you have to return his down payment plus all the house payments he made while he was living there. He's requesting all the furniture and you've agreed to his request. Based on his salary,

I'm only going to require him to give one hundred dollars a month for each child. I don't see how you're going to be able to replace the furniture. Do you see this as a fair settlement?"

"I don't care about the furniture, Your Honor."

"In that case, divorce granted." The judge pounded the gavel and looked out over the courtroom. "Next," he said in loud voice to no one in particular.

I stepped down from the witness stand and walked into the hallway. My arms and legs were shaking. I felt disconnected from myself.

I felt lighter than air and more weighed down that I'd ever been in my life. There was pain and pressure in my chest, but also a sense of exhilaration. I collapsed onto the first empty bench I could find.

"That's it," I asked my attorney. "It's over? He's not going to get custody of the girls?"

"Anne, normally I make it a point to never make negative comments about spouses in a divorce case. But I'm going to make an exception in this one. I don't like your husband. I haven't from the beginning. There's no way he's ever going to get custody of your children as long as I'm alive. He called me once to tell me he intended to file a custody suit and I felt compelled to tell him exactly what I thought his chances of winning were with me in the picture. Regardless of what he told you, he never wanted full custody of your kids. He only wanted to make your life miserable. And no, it's not quite over. Legally, your divorce won't be final for another ten months so you can't run out and get married just yet, but other than that you're a free woman. Now you'll have to excuse me. I have another case in a courthouse across town and I'm running late. My office will stay in contact with you." With a smile and a handshake he was gone.

I got up and walked towards the elevators. I felt stronger now. The worst was over. I had filed for divorce, the judge had heard my case and Bob wasn't going to get the girls. The smell of freedom was getting stronger. I left the courthouse and broke into a run as I headed towards the parking lot. "I'm free," I shouted to row after row of parked cars. "Free," I yelled to the sky as I opened my car door. "Free," I said to the emptiness the surrounded me as I put my head down on the steering wheel and sobbed.

And life went on.

When the live-in housekeeper quit, I got a new one. I went through six housekeepers in the first year alone.

When my car broke down on the freeway, I got it towed —then got it fixed.

When they had an opening at the hospital for the day shift I took it. On my days off I worked to make the extra money I needed to make the bills. Bob continued bombarding me with phone calls and we argued just as much as we ever did, but over time, his phone calls diminished until eventually they stopped altogether.

The first year after the divorce Bob added more weight to his already bulky frame and his thick black hair turned salt-and-pepper gray. He stayed busy at the church, but nothing else seemed to be coming in.

I was making new friends at work, stayed in therapy, and week by week I felt myself getting stronger.

I got a loan from the bank and repaid Linda.

If life as a free woman wasn't easy, it was at least manageable.

Two years after my divorce I decided I wanted to try living my life without the aid of a therapist.

"I've made a decision I hope you'll support," I said one Thursday morning at my regular appointment time.

"Oh?"

"I've decided I'd really like to try life on my own."

"You are on your own."

"Yes, I know. But I think I'm strong enough now and I'd like to cut down the number of times I see you."

"You mean you'd like to clean house."

"Clean house? I don't understand."

"You got rid of Bob and now you'd like to get rid of me. You're cleaning house. Getting rid of all your garbage."

His remark confused and temporarily stunned me. "What are you talking about? I never said you were garbage! I just want to reduce the number of times I come to see you."

Anger flashed through the therapist's eyes. "You know something? When you first came here you didn't have one single thought or idea of your own. Every word that came out of your mouth was what Bob said or what Bob did. I literally put you together and now you want to leave? You used me, Anne."

I exploded. "Used you? How can you say that? You're a doctor. All I did was rent space in your brain. It's your job to help people. That's what you were trained for and that's what you get paid to do. Besides, I think I had a few thoughts and ideas of my own when I came here. And even if I didn't—so what? I'm sorry you feel used, but as far as I'm concerned you were only doing your job. I think this whole response of yours really weird and it's making me uncomfortable."

"You still have issues to deal with."

"I know that. But who doesn't? Besides, I want to start figuring some of this stuff out on my own because I'm tired of being broke all the time."

An awkward silence followed.

"You may reduce your sessions to every other week."

"Fine, then that's what I'll do."

After that it was never the same.

One month later I terminated my visits. "I don't think I'll make an appointment for next week. Let's just see how I do. I'll call you if I run into trouble."

"Anne, you're not done yet. Again, I'm going to remind you that you have serious issues that still need to be resolved."

"You're probably right." I turned and smiled before closing the door behind me.

I never spoke to him again. It had ended badly and I didn't know why. I still had work to do in therapy. I knew that. But for reasons I couldn't really explain, I wanted out. Yes my budget was tight, but that was nothing new. And yes, I really did want to try life on my own, but I never could get myself to believe that was the real reason. So maybe he was right, after all. Maybe I was housecleaning. Or maybe I thought he was getting too close. Or maybe, just maybe, I didn't want to work on the incest dream—ever.

Years later, I would tell yet another therapist, "I'm not sure what happened the first time around. I know he saved my life. It just ended really badly. That's all."

Whatever my reasons were for ending the therapy, the immediate relief I felt over not having any more therapy bills was enormous.

I gave up the extra hours I'd been working and returned to Sunday morning worship services at my church.

The girls were now forced to split their time between the two churches, and although they liked going to Bel-Air, they never lost their allegiance to Bob's church, and clearly he had been right about one thing: the whole church was on his side.

On the one hand it was hard to live with the knowledge that everyone in Bob's church, except Pastor Welling, thought I was dead wrong, but on the other hand I found it oddly comforting. At least I never had to worry about the girls when they were with their father. There was always an abundance of available people in his congregation delighted to assist in babysitting.

I still had very little money and in order to make the much-needed improvements on the house. I bought handyman books. I taught myself to lay tile, paint and hang wallpaper. After putting in a new kitchen floor, I painted the house inside and out. As a teenager I'd routinely mowed lawns in the neighborhood to earn extra money and I now found that my old skills came in handy.

I fancied myself a true Renaissance woman. And if I was alone, I was alone living with a sense of victory. I was surviving on my own.

A year after the divorce Bob's hair turned white. Kim and Tina told me he was sad most of the time and still didn't understand why we'd gotten divorced, but they also said he'd started to date and they liked his new girlfriend.

In addition to every other weekend, the children spent all the major holidays with him. I thought it was only fair. After all, I reasoned, he was the one with all the relatives and extended church family, not me. I volunteered for the Thanksgiving, Christmas and New Year's Eve shifts at the hospital. It worked out well all the way around. Bob got the girls. I got the extra money, and the hospital got the much-needed help at holiday time.

My friends from work invited me to parties and occasionally I would go, but I was still shy around the men, and generally found reason to leave early.

Six months after my divorce became final I was on duty in the Intensive Care Unit on New Year's Eve when the Emergency Room doctor and nurse arrived with a patient. The nurse left as soon as the admission procedure was completed, but the doctor stayed.

"Hi. I'm Garrett Anderson. I don't usually transport patients, but we're short staffed. I haven't seen you before. Are you new here at the hospital?"

I felt my face burn red hot. "Ah . . . no."

"Well, you sure got stuck with a lousy shift."

I looked away and reached for a chart. "Oh, it's okay."

"Look, I've got to run. Let's do coffee later on. I'll call you when I get a break and maybe we can meet in the cafeteria?"

I felt awkward, uncomfortable, excited and speechless. I nodded my head and smiled.

I watched him leave and felt my heart take a leap. He was tall, slender and blonde. He didn't look anything like Bob at all. I could hardly believe my good fortune.

"Anne! You've got a date," teased one of the staff nurses.

"It's not a date. I'm only going for coffee."

But it was a date. And with that one simple gesture, I had rejoined the living.

And life went on . . .

Over the years I saw less and less of Bob, and by the time the girls were teenagers the court ordered "every other weekend" had become a thing of the past.

Vacations were still very much a part of their summer routine, however, and it was while they were on a special trip to Hawaii that Kim called from Honolulu. She was concerned. "Dad's not feeling well. He says something's not right. His chest and stomach hurt. We're coming home."

The last time I saw him, he lay dying in a county hospital.

I'd gone to see him only under duress. When the doctor called early that morning to say they needed a Do Not Resuscitate order, I'd told him to call someone else. The doctor responded, "Bob told us he wanted you."

He'd been diagnosed with pancreatic cancer after he returned from Hawaii, and by the time I saw him obstructive jaundice had turned his body an intense lime green.

Surrounded by the bleached whiteness of the hospital sheets he appeared to give off an almost incandescent glow. It was a heart-wrenching meeting. He spoke only of regret and wanting another chance at life. "I'd do so many things differently, Annie. So many."

Get-well cards, stacked high on his bedside, came from concerned church members and people high in the ecclesiastical circles. But when I pointed this out to him, he was too weak to respond. He'd wanted fame from the world through his music and God had given him fame through his music from the church.

It was a gift he never wanted. And finally, a blessing he was never able to receive. Overwhelmed by sadness and grief, I sat at his bedside and wept. Two days later, while the girls were at school, he died.

I was only one of a thousand people who attended his funeral, and the depth of my grief surprised me. There'd been so many years filled with anger and pain, so few filled with forgiveness and love.

But in the weeks and months that followed, a new understanding began to seep its way into my heart. Slowly, ever so slowly, I began to understand that the grief I felt was not for our love that had died so many years before.

My grief was for a lifetime of worn out hopes. My pain was for all the dreams that had burned with such white-hot intensity when we were young and that flickered in my heart, still. What would become of all our dreams now? Now that death had taken the final embers away. "You promised me. You promised me. You promised me . . . " I cried to an empty room and no one at all.

And life went on. And the years passed . . .

My memories are part of me now and having spent more years in therapy than I care to admit, I no longer refer to my life as "this is the good part" or "this is the bad." My life is simply my life.

And it is my belief that God was always there for me, even in my darkest hours. For how else do you explain these feelings I have? Feelings of satisfaction in knowing that somehow through God's forgiveness and grace I have not only survived my life—I have prevailed. And feelings of joy in knowing that life is basically good even if there are times when it doesn't make any sense.

It has taken me a lifetime but I know now that my heart has always been on a journey to learn how to love and to forgive . . . myself.

Epilogue

Kim's beaded pearl and sequined dress made of white silk organza suddenly billowed when the ushers opened the sanctuary doors. Kim looked so beautiful that when she saw her walking down the aisle she thought, just for a moment, her heart would stop. Kim chose to come down the aisle alone. Many, including her step-father, had volunteered to escort her but she felt that no one could take her father's place. It was a sad, courageous and ultimately beautiful gesture to the man who had truly been her father, but never a parent.

Over four hundred people filled Bel-Air Presbyterian Church that Saturday morning in July. Most of the guests were Kim's friends from UCLA where she'd met her future husband and where she spent her days as an on-campus minister. Tina declined to sing, even though she'd just finished working several months with Elton John on his new musical *Aida*. "Kimmy," she said with the wisdom of the world in her voice, "I cried my eyes out when they called your name at your college graduation. There's no hope I'll ever get through your wedding."

Instead, dressed in a floor-length, lavender, silk chiffon dress with her auburn hair flowing down onto her shoulders, Tina chose to stand next to her sister and hold Kim's flowers as she said her vows.

Few who attended the wedding even knew that Kim had almost lost her life in a fire or that Tina had been born with so many birth defects. It was as if those events had been placed in the family attic. Not hidden . . . just stored.

Her parents did not attend, though they were invited.

Nothing in her relationship with them had changed much over the years. They did, however, manage to develop a rather strange ritual. One year, after she'd remarried, they sent her a poinsettia plant at Christmas. The following year, knowing how much they enjoyed cheese, she sent them a Holiday gift basket from Wisconsin, the cheese capital of the world. And after that it just fell into a pattern. Every Christmas she'd send them a basket of cheese and every Christmas they'd send her a poinsettia plant. But that was it. In the end, her entire relationship with her parents came down to a poinsettia plant and a basket of cheese.

Eventually, she returned to therapy to deal with the issue of incest, but she never spoke of it to her parents. She'd been told by those close to her father that his tendency towards violence remained—even after all these years.

She remarried and stayed in the church, even though over the years well-meaning friends have encouraged her to leave. "What has the church ever done for you except bring you heartache and pain?" they ask with genuine sincerity.

But she stayed. She stayed because her love affair with God that began as a five-year-old child still lives in her heart today. And she knows that she has survived her life and now lives with a sense of victory, all by the grace of God.

About the Author

A retired nurse, Anita Swanson has studied non-fiction writing with numerous writing programs, including the UCLA Writers Program and the prestigious University of Iowa Writing Program. She is currently an active member of the International Women's Writing Guild. Her work has been published in *Whispers from Heaven, The Chrysalis Reader,* and the anthology of short stories, *Ship's Log: Writings at Sea.*

Married for sixteen years, Ms. Swanson writes and resides in Lake County, California, where she attends First Baptist Church of Lakeport.